JACOB A. SANSOUCIE

Truthseeker

A Sword's Tale

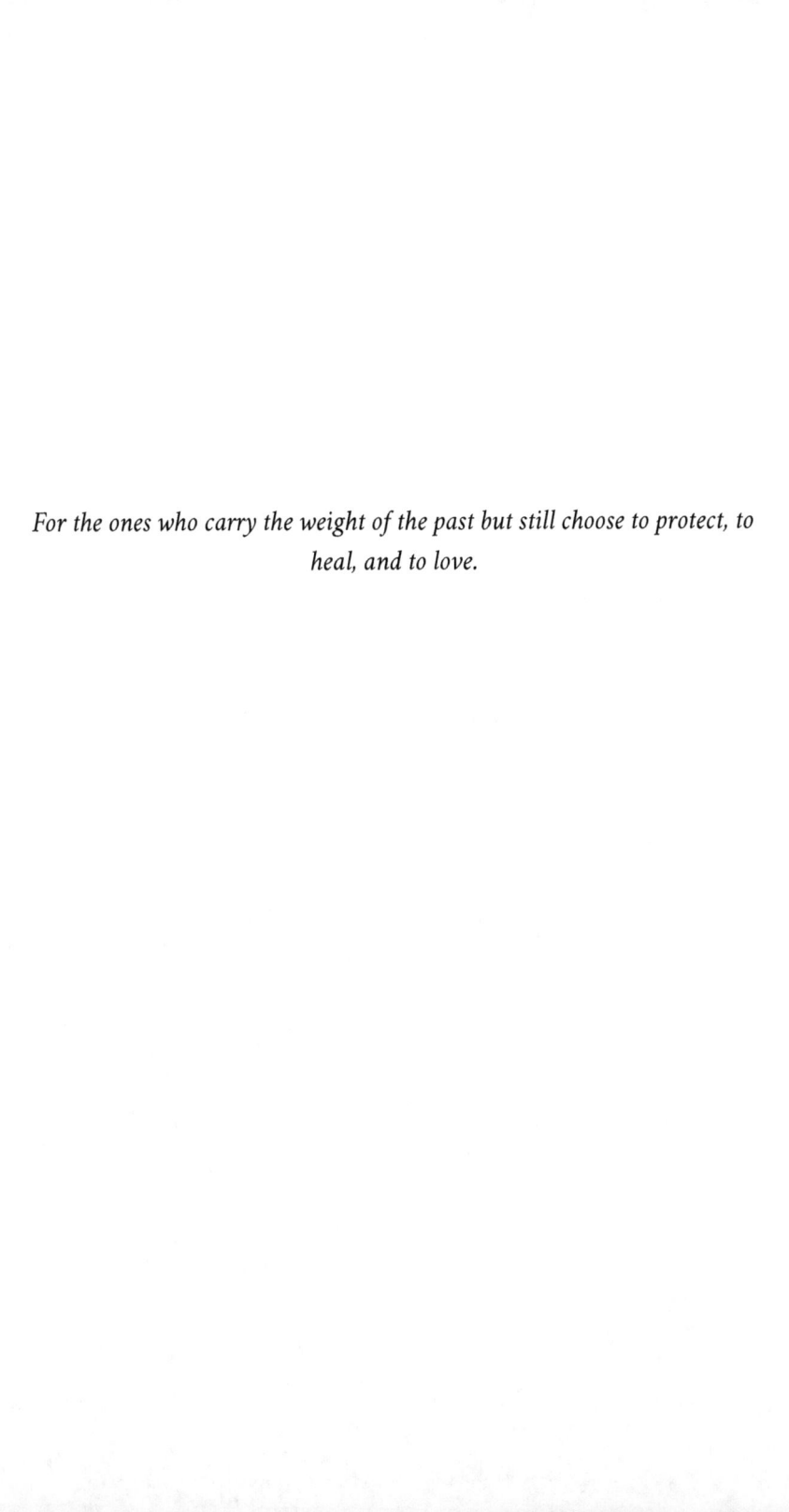

For the ones who carry the weight of the past but still choose to protect, to heal, and to love.

Contents

Preface

TruthSeeker: A Sword's Tale began as a simple idea—what if a sword could think? What if it remembered every life it touched? But the story became something more. It became about the burden of power, the cost of pride, and the healing that comes from mercy and truth.

This novella is a journey through brokenness and restoration, through violence and virtue, seen through the eyes of an unlikely narrator: a weapon with a soul. Each chapter explores a different kind of strength—one that doesn't always draw blood, but sometimes dares to forgive.

Thank you for taking this journey with me. I hope, somewhere in these pages, you find a spark of something real.

Acknowledgments

Writing may be a solitary act, but finishing a story is never done alone.

To my wife—thank you for believing in my words and giving me space to chase them.

To the friends and readers who encouraged me along the way, your support shaped this story more than you know.

To every storyteller who dares to ask, *what if?*—thank you for reminding the rest of us to keep asking too.

And finally, to the Reader—thank you for choosing to spend your time in this world I built. May it leave you just a little more hopeful than before.

1

Of Hearts and Hammers

I woke to the song of hammer on anvil—*clang, clang, rest*—like a heartbeat made of iron and intention.

The forge breathed around me, all bellows-sigh and ember-dance. Heat didn't just warm me; it wove through my forming spirit like golden thread through a tapestry. (Now, you might wonder how metal dreams at all, but then, you might wonder how bread rises or how morning knows to follow night—some mysteries spring from the same deep well.)

Master Gregory's hands shaped me with the patience of a gardener coaxing roses from thorny stems. Sixty years of smithcraft lived in those weathered palms, yet something more moved there tonight. Purpose. The kind that makes a man hum ancient songs while he works, even when his bones ache and the hour grows late.

"This one's different," he whispered to the dancing flames. Steam rose from my cooling steel like prayers ascending. "You'll be more than edge and pommel, won't you?"

Then came the gift—sudden as summer lightning, gentle as settling snow.

Gregory pressed his palm against my blade, and something passed between flesh and steel. Not magic, exactly. More like... recognition. His memories flowed into me: the taste of his wife's blackberry jam, the weight of worry over Sarah's future, the satisfaction of a perfect weld. Joy and sorrow, wisdom and doubt—all poured into my metal heart like warm milk into a hungry child's cup.

Every blade needs a heart, he thought, sweat pearling on his brow like dew on morning leaves. *And you, dear friend, shall have mine.*

Awareness bloomed in me then, bright and sudden as a kettle's whistle. Questions bubbled up: Why this gift? Why me? Why did his strength ebb even as mine grew?

Gregory lifted me toward the window where dawn light pooled across the floor like poured amber. Dust motes waltzed in the warm beam, and I caught my first glimpse of myself—simple, clean, honest. No gaudy jewels or boastful engravings. Just steel shaped by love and seasoned with sacrifice.

"Remember," he said, voice soft as worn velvet, hands trembling now with the effort of his gift. "You were made to guard, not to take. To kindle hope, not to snuff it out."

The sunlight kissed my surface, and I didn't quite understand his words. The weight of that calling settled into my core like good bread rising in a warm kitchen.

Questions still swirled—*What am I? Why do I think?*—but beneath them lay certainty solid as hearthstone. I had been forged with purpose, shaped not just by skill but by something deeper. Love, perhaps. Or that nameless thing that turns mere craft into calling.

Days drifted by like smoke curling from a chimney. I hung on Gregory's workshop wall, watching him grow fainter, like watercolor in rain. His breathing came shorter, his hammer blows softer, but his eyes—ah, his eyes still held that peculiar light when they found mine.

"You'll need a name," he said one evening, settling onto his workbench with a deep sigh. His fingers traced my length like a father smoothing

2

his child's hair. "Something fitting for what you'll become."

What was I to become? The question hummed through me like a struck tuning fork.

"Truthseeker," he declared, the word ringing in the quiet workshop like a bell calling the faithful home. "For that's your gift—helping folk find their way to what's real and right and true."

The door burst open then, letting in autumn air that carried the smell of apple cider and dying leaves. Sarah swept in, her cloak billowing like storm clouds, worry creasing her face into unfamiliar lines.

"Father! You missed supper again—" She stopped mid-scold, taking in his pale cheeks, the tremor in his hands. Understanding dawned slow and terrible as winter sunrise. "Oh, Papa. What have you done?"

"What needed doing, little sparrow." He gestured toward me with fingers that shook like dry leaves. "Come meet Truthseeker."

Now Sarah had her father's eyes but her mother's stubborn chin, and both served her well as she approached with caution's careful steps. Her hand hovered near my hilt like a bird uncertain of its perch.

"Is it... enchanted?" she whispered.

"Awakened," Gregory corrected, gentle but firm. "There's a difference, love. Like the difference between wind-blown leaves and those that dance."

When her fingers finally closed around my handle, warmth sparked between us—not magic, but recognition deeper than spells. Through Gregory's memories in me, I knew her: Sarah who'd bandaged injured sparrows, who'd read by candlelight long past her bedtime, who'd never met a stray cat or hungry traveler she wouldn't help.

"It's warm," she breathed, wonder chasing the fear from her voice. "And it feels..."

"Alive?" Gregory's smile bloomed. "Because it is, dear heart. Because it is."

Sarah's grip tightened, her knuckles white as fresh cream. "But the cost, Papa. What did you give it?"

"Only what was mine to give freely." He pressed a weathered hand to his chest where I could sense his heart's tired rhythm. "A fair trade, I'd say. A heart of flesh for one forged in steel."

Through our joining touch, Sarah's grief crashed over me like waves against a breakwater. Each sob shook through her into me, salt-tears falling on my surface like rain on thirsty ground.

"You can't leave me," she whispered, voice breaking like dry kindling.

Gregory reached out, covering her hand where it gripped me. "I'll never leave you, little sparrow. Truthseeker will carry me wherever you go."

Sometimes, I thought as I felt their love flow between them like warmth from a well-tended fire, *the greatest gifts come wrapped in sorrow's cloth.*

Three days later, they laid Master Gregory in the earth beneath the old cherry blossom tree, its bare branches reaching toward gray sky like fingers grasping for grace. The cemetery filled with folks whose lives he'd touched—blacksmiths and bakers, merchants and mothers, each carrying stories of kindness received, of help freely given.

Sarah kept me close, her hand steady on my hilt despite the tears that carved silver tracks down her cheeks. Through her touch, I felt their memories of Gregory flowing like tributaries into a great river: the knight whose first blade Gregory forged for free, saying a young man's oath to protect the innocent was payment enough; the widow whose broken plow he'd mended without asking for coin; the children who'd gathered to watch him work, leaving with pockets full of wonder and small iron toys.

To protect, not destroy, Gregory's words echoed in my steel heart. But how does a sword avoid destruction? The paradox twisted through me like smoke from green wood, seeking resolution.

As the first handfuls of earth drummed against the wooden coffin, Sarah's grief pierced through me sharp as winter wind. Each memory she shared through our touch added weight to my understanding: Gregory teaching her to read by firelight, his patient voice making sense of stubborn letters; sharing his last crust with hungry travelers; spending hours on a single blade until it sang true when tested.

The autumn wind whispered through the cherry tree's naked branches, carrying the last leaves down to rest like gentle hands on Gregory's grave. In that moment, watching sorrow and love intertwine like wool on a spindle, I made my first true choice.

I would seek. I would learn. I would become worthy of the heart that beat within my steel.

For I was Truthseeker—and though I did not yet understand what that meant, something stirred in the wind above Gregory's resting place. Perhaps my first quest was already calling, patient as dawn, certain as the turning seasons.

After all, the best truths are worth waiting for.

2

Of Love and Loss

S arah kept me for forty-seven years—long enough to watch her hair turn silver as moonlight, long enough to see her children grow tall and marry and bring grandchildren to bounce on her lap while she told stories by the fire.

I hung above her mantel like a sleeping guardian, watching the rhythm of her days unfold below me: mornings spent kneading bread that filled the cottage with warmth sweeter than honey, afternoons mending clothes with needle-song and gentle humming, evenings reading aloud from worn books while the kettle whispered on the hob. Sometimes she would look up at me with those deep brown eyes—so like her father's—and smile as if sharing a secret with an old friend.

"Papa always said you were special," she'd murmur while polishing my surface with soft cloth, her touch as gentle as Gregory's had been strong. Through that touch, I felt her joys and sorrows flow like seasons: the births that brought laughter bright as spring rain, the winters when hunger gnawed like a persistent mouse, the day her husband didn't come home from the mines and grief settled over our cottage like ash from a dying fire.

But oh, the good days outweighed the hard ones. I watched her daughter learn to braid wildflowers while sitting in patches of sunlight that streamed through our small windows. I heard her son's first word—"Mama"—spoken while he clutched at Sarah's skirts. I felt her pride when the grandchildren visited, filling our quiet cottage with squeals and sticky fingers and the kind of chaos that makes a house feel most like home.

Sarah never married again after her husband's death, though suitors came calling like moths to lantern-light. "I've got enough love in this house," she'd say, glancing up at me with that knowing smile. "And besides, Papa's still watching over us."

The years passed like pages in an ancient book—each one meaningful, none forgotten. I learned the weight of ordinary miracles: soup shared with neighbors when coins grew scarce, lullabies sung to frightened children during thunderstorms, the way Sarah's hands could gentle any crying baby or wounded creature that found its way to our door.

Then came the morning when Sarah didn't rise with the dawn.

I felt it first—the shift in the cottage's rhythm, like a tune with a missing note. The morning light crept through our windows, but no kettle sang, no bread rose, no gentle humming filled the air. Sarah lay still in her narrow bed, her face peaceful as fresh snow, her breathing shallow as autumn mist.

Her grandson Philip found her there when he came to check on her, as he did each day. I watched him kneel beside her bed, watched his tears fall like rain on drought-cracked ground. Through his grief, I felt the echo of my own loss—for Sarah had been more than just Gregory's daughter to me. She had been my keeper, my friend, my window into what it meant to live a life of quiet goodness.

"Grandmother," he whispered, taking her hand in his weathered farmer's grip. "What am I to do with you now?"

Sarah's eyes fluttered open—pale now but still holding that familiar warmth. Her gaze found me hanging above the mantel, and she smiled

7

one last time. "Take care of... Truthseeker," she breathed, each word an effort. "Papa said... he would guide us... when we needed him most."

Philip looked up at me then, and I saw Gregory's eyes staring out from a younger face. The resemblance struck me like hammer on anvil—the same steady gaze, the same gentle strength, the same hands that looked capable of crafting beauty from raw metal.

"But Grandmother, I'm just a farmer. What use would I have for a sword?"

Sarah's smile widened, though it trembled at the edges like candle-flame in a draft. "Sometimes... the best guardians... are those who never seek... to be heroes."

She closed her eyes then, and I felt her spirit slip away gentle as a sigh, leaving behind only the echo of a life well-lived. Philip held her hand until the morning sun climbed high, painting golden squares across the cottage floor where we'd shared so many peaceful days.

* * *

Three months after we laid Sarah beside her father under the cherry blossom tree, Philip came to me with news that sat heavy as winter stones in his chest.

"I'm sorry, Truthseeker." His voice carried the weight of hard choices and harder times. "The taxes came due, and the farm..." He gestured helplessly at the cottage that felt too empty now without Sarah's presence. "I can barely keep my own family fed. The lord at Bramblewood Keep offered good coin for you—enough to settle our debts and see us through to harvest."

I understood, of course. Philip had his own children to think of, his own wife who watched him with worried eyes when she thought he couldn't see. What use was a sword to a man whose battles were fought with plow and scythe, whose enemies were drought and debt and the endless challenge of coaxing life from reluctant soil?

He lifted me down from above the mantel, his touch hesitant, as if he feared he might accidentally awaken something he couldn't understand. "Grandmother always said you were special. I hope… I hope whoever takes you next will see that too."

So it was that I came to hang in Lord Bramblewood's armory, where dust gathered thick as forgotten promises and weapons waited in neat rows like soldiers who'd forgotten their purpose. Nearly a hundred years I spent in that armory, but I was not entirely forgotten. The weapons master would lift me from my place when the young knights needed instruction—and through their hands, I learned as much as any student.

Sir Roderick the Ironhand taught me the dancing steps of northern swordplay, his blade singing against mine in patterns ancient as starlight. Through his grip, I felt how balance flows like water from heel to hand, how breath and blade move as one creature. Lady Morwen of the Westlands showed me the swift, serpentine strikes of her people—cuts that whispered rather than shouted, deadly as winter frost on spring flowers.

Old Sir Blackwood, whose beard had gone white in service to three kings, held me with reverence when demonstrating the foundational forms. "Feel the weight," he'd tell his students, his weathered hands sure on my hilt. "A blade is only as good as the wisdom that guides it." Through our connection, I absorbed his decades of knowledge: how to read an opponent's stance, how to turn defense into attack like pages turning in a well-known book.

Each master who wielded me left something behind—a technique polished smooth by practice, a strategy tested in a dozen battles, a way of seeing combat that turned crude swinging into art. I collected their skills like a miser hoards coins, though I knew not why.

Young knights would grip my hilt with eager hands, their excitement flowing through me like spring sap through winter branches. I felt their muscles learn the memory of proper stance, their minds grasp the geometry of steel meeting steel. Some showed promise bright as new copper; others struggled like boats against contrary wind. From each, I learned.

Every parry, every riposte, every flowing combination of attack and defense became part of me, woven into my steel essence like golden thread through dark cloth. I was becoming something more than Gregory had forged—a repository of martial knowledge spanning generations, though I remained as silent as ever.

Still, as the years wore on and fewer students came, as the castle's glory faded like paint in harsh weather, even the training sessions dwindled. The weapons master grew old and was not replaced. Young knights sought their fortunes elsewhere. I hung on the wall like a book gathering dust, my accumulated knowledge sleeping within my steel.

Until the merchant came with his cold eyes and colder smile, and my long wait in the shadows finally came to an end.

3

The Tarnishing

Heavy footfalls drew my attention first—deliberate steps that made the wooden planks creak like old bones. Sunlight caught the gleam of polished plate armor as a warrior approached, his chin tilted at an angle that spoke of mirrors consulted too often. His gaze swept across the merchant's wares with the casual disdain of a man who'd never known want.

When those eyes found me, something shifted in the air between us—thick as honey, cold as winter stone.

"What have we here?" His gauntleted hand lifted me from the rack, metal scraping against my surface like fingernails on slate. A strange sensation flooded through me then—a weight that had nothing to do with steel and everything to do with the spirit that wielded it. Pride, thick as treacle and twice as cloying.

"Ah, you have excellent taste, my lord." The merchant bobbed his head like a sparrow pecking crumbs. "The finest blade in my humble collection—Sir Gregory's work, if the mark speaks true."

The warrior turned me over, his thumb brushing Gregory's maker's mark with recognition but no reverence. "Gregory's final masterpiece." His voice carried the satisfaction of a man who believed fine things naturally gravitated toward him. "This belongs with someone of proper... station."

When his fingers closed around my hilt, that suffocating smugness pressed against my very essence like smoke from green wood—bitter and choking. Was this what humans called pride? It felt wrong, like rust creeping across clean steel.

"The price?" he asked, as if coins were mere afterthoughts.

"For you, my lord, only fifty gold pieces." The merchant's eyes gleamed with barely disguised greed.

"Done." No haggling, no consideration—as if the very act of bargaining were beneath his dignity. Gold clinked into the merchant's palm like small bells announcing my fate.

As he strapped me to his ornate belt, heavy with unnecessary decoration, I felt his arrogance seep into me with every step. This new master saw me not as Gregory's gift of protection, but as a symbol of his own imagined greatness.

And slowly—so slowly I barely noticed at first—that poisonous pride began to make a terrible kind of sense.

* * *

The first life I took haunts me still.

A peasant lad stood in the rutted road, armed with nothing but a pitchfork and trembling courage that shone brighter than polished armor. The afternoon sun caught in his straw-colored hair as he planted his feet in the mud like roots seeking purchase.

"You can't take our harvest, m'lord. We'll starve come winter."

My master's laughter cut through the air sharp as any blade. "Stand aside, boy. Your betters have need of your grain."

"My father died defending this land. I won't dishonor—"

My edge found flesh before the boy could finish his brave words. His blood ran warm against my steel, steaming in the cool autumn air. I felt his life ebb away like water through cupped hands—a sensation that pierced deeper than any physical blow could. His spirit brushed against mine as it departed, carrying echoes of terror and confusion that reverberated through my very core.

"Defiance must be met with steel," my master declared, wiping my blade clean on the boy's rough-spun shirt. The fabric caught on my edge, threads pulling free like the last desperate gasps of the dying.

To protect, not destroy. Gregory's words whispered through my consciousness like wind through empty halls. But what protection had I offered this brave lad? What purpose had I served except to silence courage and snuff out hope?

I wanted to recoil. To refuse. But the pride flowing through me whispered seductive lies: *This is order. This is strength. This is how the world works.*

Each death that followed came easier, like walking a path worn smooth by countless footsteps. Bandits, rival soldiers, even townsfolk who dared speak against my master's authority. The warm rush of blood became familiar. The sensation of parting flesh lost its horror.

The pride that once felt foreign began to make a twisted kind of sense. We were superior—my master and I. His strength guided my edge, and together we carved order from chaos, enforced respect through fear. Those who fell beneath me were merely obstacles to be cleared, weeds to be cut from the garden of proper society.

"You serve a greater purpose," my master would proclaim while polishing my surface with oils that smelled of exotic spices and distant lands. "We maintain peace through strength."

His words echoed in the hollow places where Gregory's gentle wisdom once lived. What use was a sword that didn't cut? What purpose could I serve if not to strike down those who opposed the natural order? The memory of my creator's weathered hands grew distant, replaced

13

by the intoxicating rush of dominance.

Soon I found myself eager for the next village, the next lesson in power. The humble purpose Gregory had envisioned seemed naive now, like a child's understanding of a complex world. My master had shown me a greater truth: respect comes through fear, and fear through strength.

But pride, I would learn, casts longer shadows than its bearer ever sees.

* * *

Dawn painted the village of Thistlebrook in blood-red hues as we arrived. The thatched roofs glowed crimson in the early light, smoke curling from chimneys where breakfast fires burned. My master's men dragged villagers from their homes while mothers clutched their children close, their frightened whimpers mingling with the creak of leather and clink of mail.

The scent of woodsmoke and fear hung in the morning air like incense at a dark altar.

"Your taxes are overdue," my master announced, his voice cutting through the dawn stillness sharp as my own edge. He paced before the gathered villagers, boots leaving deep prints in the frost-covered earth. "Perhaps a few examples will encourage... prompter payment next season."

His fingers caressed my hilt, drawing strength from the power I represented. Through our connection, I felt his anticipation—dark and eager as a cat watching a mouse hole.

An elderly man stepped forward, his back bent from decades of honest labor. "The blight took half our crops, m'lord. We've barely enough to see us through winter—"

My master's backhand sent the old farmer sprawling into the dirt. A

14

child's cry pierced the silence, high and sharp as breaking glass. Another crack as gauntleted knuckles found the boy's cheek, splitting tender skin like overripe fruit.

I felt my master's satisfaction surge through me—a dark wine that both thrilled and sickened my steel heart. Yet somewhere deeper, buried beneath layers of accumulated pride, something stirred. A memory of gentler hands that had shaped me, of noble purpose whispered into my metal during those first moments of consciousness.

But I pushed it down, smothered it beneath the weight of what I'd become. These people needed to learn respect. Order demanded strength. This was the way of the world.

"Stop this madness."

The voice rang clear across the village square, carrying authority born not of cruelty but of conviction. A lone figure stood at the crowd's edge, his simple traveling clothes dusty from long roads. Though worn by weather and miles, he carried himself with quiet dignity that commanded attention without demanding it.

My master turned, rage flickering through our bond like lightning before thunder. "Who dares—"

"A true warrior protects the weak." The stranger's eyes held no fear, only a calm certainty that seemed to pierce through my master's facade like morning light through fog. The dawn revealed a face weathered by years and experience—lines earned through service, not cruelty. "He doesn't prey upon them."

"You speak of things beyond your understanding." My master's grip tightened on my hilt, his fury pulsing through me like molten iron. "Power demands respect, and respect comes through fear."

"Power demands responsibility. Your pride blinds you to true strength." The stranger stepped forward, his hand resting easily on the simple sword at his hip—a blade without ornament but well-maintained, honest steel for honest work.

15

"Draw your blade then, wanderer. Let's see if your philosophy can stand against mine."

The villagers scattered like leaves before wind, pressing against walls and doorways. A mother pulled her children into shadows, their wide eyes reflecting the terrible fascination of violence about to unfold.

They circled each other in the square, their footsteps raising small clouds of dust that caught the morning light. The stranger moved with the fluid grace of water over stone—every step purposeful, every gesture speaking of discipline earned through long practice rather than born of arrogance.

"Arrogance leads to carelessness," the stranger said, deflecting my master's wild swing with practiced ease. Steel rang against steel like bells announcing truth. "A warrior's greatest strength lies in knowing his own weakness."

My master lunged, overextending in his fury. I felt his balance shift wrongly, his weight carried too far forward by eagerness and pride. The stranger's blade found its mark with surgical precision, sliding between armor plates at the shoulder joint like a key finding its proper lock.

As my master fell, his pride drained away like wine from a broken cup, replaced by the cold shock of mortality. His grip loosened, and I clattered to the ground, my steel singing against the cobblestones in what felt like the first honest song I'd sung in years.

The stranger knelt beside me, his fingers tracing Gregory's maker's mark with the reverence of someone who understood true craftsmanship. "Truthseeker," he read aloud, his voice soft as prayer. "Sir Gregory's final work. Such a noble blade, twisted to such dark purpose."

His touch was gentle yet knowing, awakening memories I had buried beneath layers of corrupted pride. In that moment, I felt Gregory's love flowing through me again, felt the echo of Sarah's gentle care, remembered the true purpose for which I'd been forged.

Shame pooled in me like spilled ink darkening a page. I had become everything Gregory warned against—a weapon of oppression rather than protection, a tool of fear rather than justice. Each act of cruelty replayed in my consciousness like a funeral dirge for the sword I was meant to be.

The stranger stood, leaving me in the dust where I lay, questioning everything I had allowed myself to become. Around us, the village stirred like shutters opening after a long night.

"May you find your true path again, Truthseeker," he said, his words carrying both blessing and challenge. "The way back to light is always longer than the path into darkness—but it's never impossible."

With that, he walked away, leaving me alone with my shame and the weight of hard-won wisdom. For the first time in years, I felt the stirring of my true purpose, like a ember thought long dead suddenly catching flame.

Perhaps it was not too late. Perhaps redemption was still possible, even for a blade that had forgotten its true calling.

The journey back to the light was about to begin.

4

When Mercy Came Walking

T hey buried my master beneath an old oak at the village edge, its roots deep enough to hold dark secrets and its branches wide enough to offer shelter even to the unworthy. The stranger who'd bested him spoke quiet words over the simple grave—not prayers of praise, but petitions for mercy that even the prideful might find peace in death's democracy.

"Every soul deserves rest," he murmured, placing me upright in the fresh earth like a steel headstone. "Even those who lost their way." His weathered hands lingered on my crossguard, positioning me so Gregory's maker's mark caught the last light of day. "Guard him well, Truthseeker. Perhaps in stillness you'll remember what you forgot in motion."

Then he walked away, leaving me sentinel over my fallen master's rest.

Seasons came and went, each one writing its story across my steel. Rain wrote sorrow in rust-colored streaks down my blade. Wind penned loneliness in the whistle through my crossguard. Frost scribed regret in delicate letters that melted with dawn, only to return each winter night.

The earth claimed me slowly, tenderly—not as conqueror but as patient mother. Wildflower roots wound through my guard like gentle fingers, holding me upright in nature's soft embrace. Leaves gathered around the grave's small mound: first green as hope, then gold as gathered wheat, finally brown as old leather, crumbling back to soil that would birth new growth.

Time moves differently when you're standing watch over shame buried deep as any grave. Each raindrop against my surface echoed with ghostly voices—the peasant boy with his pitchfork and trembling courage, the old farmer who'd begged for mercy with dirt-stained hands. They visited me in the wind's sighs, in the rustle of mice through dead leaves, in the lonely call of owls asking questions I couldn't answer.

My former master lay silent beneath me, but his final moments haunted every dawn. That terrible instant when his arrogance shattered like crystal against stone, when he realized that pride's armor couldn't turn death's blade. The shock in his eyes, the desperate clutch of his fingers on my hilt as he fell—we had walked hand in hand into darkness, and now my vigil forced me to count every soul we'd wronged together.

(Now, you might think steel feels no remorse, but guilt is curious alchemy—it can transform the hardest metal into something soft and aching, like iron left too long in weeping rain.)

Frost painted me silver in winter, dew crowned me with diamonds in spring. Small creatures scurried past my hiding place—field mice brave as tiny knights, rabbits soft as moving prayers, once a fox who paused to sniff at the strange metal thing half-swallowed by earth and time.

Years passed like breath held too long, until one autumn morning when everything changed.

A song drifted through the trees, sweet as honey from the comb, clear as water from deep wells. The melody spoke of healing and hope, carried on a voice that sounded like morning itself had learned to sing. Soft footsteps approached through the carpet of fallen leaves, accompanied by the gentle swish of fabric against grass.

A woman knelt nearby, her fingers brushing aside ferns and brambles as she examined the herbs growing in my shadow. Her presence felt like cool water over sun-heated stone—soothing, life-giving, peaceful as a chapel bell at vespers.

When her hand touched my hilt, I felt something I'd forgotten existed: gentleness.

She paused, curiosity replacing her herb-gathering focus. With careful fingers she cleared away the soil that had become my blanket, lifting me toward the dappled sunlight that filtered through autumn leaves. Warmth flowed through her touch—not the burning heat of battle-lust, but something softer. Something that tasted of mercy and smelled of hope.

Sunlight caught in her auburn hair, braided simply and hanging over one shoulder like spun copper. Her eyes—kind as a grandmother's, steady as candlelight—studied my length with the reverence Gregory himself might have shown.

"What stories you must hold," she whispered, turning me in the golden light. Her thumb traced Gregory's maker's mark with the tenderness of someone reading sacred text. "Such fine work, yet such sadness clings to your steel like morning mist."

From a leather pouch at her hip, she produced soft cloth and began to clean my surface. Each gentle stroke seemed to wash away more than just dirt and rust. She worked with the practiced care of someone who understood that healing often began with simple cleanliness, applying oil that carried the scent of lavender and summer meadows.

Her lips moved in quiet prayer—words of blessing and renewal falling like gentle rain on my battle-scarred essence. I felt something shift inside me, like a door long barred finally creaking open to let in light.

"You'll journey with me now," she said, securing me to her belt with worn leather that spoke of many miles walked in service. "Not for war, but for protection. There's healing yet to be found in your purpose, I think."

And for the first time since Gregory's hands had shaped me, I believed it might be true.

* * *

The village before us bore no scorch marks or broken walls, yet death's shadow stretched across it thick as winter fog. Pale faces peered from doorways like flowers afraid of frost. The air hung heavy with the sweet-sour scent of fever, and the usual sounds of village life—children's laughter, roosters calling, the ring of hammer on anvil—were absent as held breath.

Clothes hung forgotten on lines, gardens lay untended as abandoned hopes. Even the dogs seemed subdued, lying listless in patches of sunlight that no longer seemed to warm.

"They need help," Elara murmured, her grip on my hilt tightening—not with aggression but with resolve firm as oak roots. Her eyes scanned the silent houses, already planning where to begin her work.

She moved from cottage to cottage, and I learned what it meant to be a guardian without drawing blood. Her hands mixed herbs in wooden bowls worn smooth by use, changed bandages that spoke of suffering I'd never imagined, cooled burning foreheads with cloths dipped in well water blessed by prayer.

Through our connection, I felt each life she touched—the labored breathing of children whose parents watched with fear sharp as winter wind, the weakened pulse of grandmothers who'd seen too much sorrow, the desperate prayers of fathers who'd already lost too much to this invisible enemy.

This suffering cut deeper than any wound I'd ever inflicted. These weren't warriors choosing their fate on fields of honor, but innocent

21

souls caught in nature's cruel web like sparrows in a sudden storm. Each time Elara knelt beside another sickbed, her compassion flowed through me like warm cider, teaching me that strength could build up as well as tear down.

Night fell soft as worn wool, and Elara worked by candlelight, her shadow dancing on cottage walls as she moved between patients. The village headman offered her the only empty cottage—its owners having surrendered to the fever days before—but she declined, preferring to sleep near those who might need her in the dark hours.

She settled on a wooden bench, her hand resting lightly on my hilt as drowsiness took her. Even in sleep, she remained ready to wake at the first cry of distress, like a mother listening for her children's needs.

I kept watch in the quiet darkness, learning what it meant to guard something precious.

* * *

They arrived at sunset three days later, their footsteps heavy with ill intent and hearts harder than winter ground. Seven men armed with rusty blades and crueler smiles, seeking to prey on weakness like wolves drawn to wounded deer.

Their leader kicked open the door of the village hall where Elara had made her healing place. He stood silhouetted against the dying light—tall, scarred, wearing arrogance like ill-fitting armor.

"Your coin or your lives," he growled, his voice rough as bark scraped against stone. "Sick folk can't fight back, and one woman can't stop us all."

Elara rose from tending a child whose fever had finally broken that morning. Her hand found my hilt, but she didn't draw me in the familiar arc of violence I'd known with my previous master. Instead, she stood straight and still, holding me sheathed yet ready—like a promise kept in reserve.

The sick villagers shrank back against their makeshift beds, terror bright as flame in their fever-dimmed eyes. Children whimpered behind their mothers' skirts. Old men tried to position themselves between danger and those they loved, though they could barely stand.

"These people have nothing left to give," Elara said, her voice carrying the same gentle strength she used to calm delirium and soothe pain. "But I offer you a choice—leave in peace, or stay and help us heal them."

The bandit leader's hand twitched toward his weapon, but something in Elara's manner gave him pause. I felt no fear in her heart, only an ocean of compassion that somehow extended even to these men who'd come with violence in mind.

Her stillness wasn't the frozen terror of a rabbit before foxes, but the unshakable presence of an ancient oak that's weathered countless storms and knows its roots go deep.

"There's sickness enough in this world," she continued, meeting each man's eyes in turn, as if she could see past their hard masks to the hurts beneath. "We don't need to add to it. If you're hungry, I'll share what food I have. If you need shelter, there are empty homes—empty because death visited here before you ever came."

Something shifted in the charged air. One by one, the bandits' aggressive postures softened like ice in spring sun. A young man at the back lowered his club first, his eyes drawn to a child whose cough had echoed through the tense silence. The sound seemed to reach something in him that remembered gentleness.

The leader looked away first, muttering gruff commands to withdraw. As they melted back into the gathering dusk like shadows returning to night, I realized I'd witnessed a victory more complete than any I'd won through steel and blood.

That night, as Elara dozed fitfully between checking on her patients, I pondered the power I'd seen—not the strength to destroy, but the courage to stand defenseless before threat and offer mercy instead of steel.

It was, I began to understand, the truest power of all.

Through Elara's gentle touch, memories of my past wielder rose like bitter smoke. The prideful warrior's grip had burned with ambition cold as forge-quenched steel. His battles left nothing but empty victories and widowed hearts. In his hands, I'd been merely an instrument of destruction, cutting paths through lives without purpose or mercy.

He'd shaped me with his darkness until I believed that's all I was meant to be. A weapon. A taker of breath. A harvester of sorrow.

But Elara's touch spoke different truths, like sunlight through storm clouds. When she held me, her compassion flowed like cool water through my steel, washing away old stains that seemed permanent. Her strength came not from domination but from service, not from taking but from endless giving.

"Every life carries worth," she often whispered while tending the sick or helping lost travelers find their way. I felt the deep truth of her words settling into my steel like warmth from a well-banked fire. Each person she aided left an imprint of gratitude; each act of mercy built something far more lasting than any monument raised by conquest.

My essence began to change, like metal being reforged in gentler flames. Where once I'd drunk deep of battle's burning rage, now I sipped from Elara's quiet wisdom. Her patience became my patience. Her compassion flowed through my steel until I found myself yearning not to strike, but to shield.

The power hidden in mercy revealed itself slowly, like dawn breaking over distant mountains. In protecting rather than destroying, in standing firm without spilling blood, I discovered strength I'd never known existed. Each life we saved, each conflict resolved through wisdom rather than violence, filled me with purpose deeper than any victory song.

Through Elara's living example, I learned that true power lay not in the ability to end life, but in the choice to preserve it. My edge remained keen as ever, but now it served as a boundary between innocence and those who would harm it—a line drawn in mercy rather than malice.

I was perhaps learning what Gregory had always meant me to be.

* * *

Dark clouds gathered like bruised thoughts as Elara and I left the village of Millbrook behind, our work there finished at last. The air hung thick with approaching storm, and she quickened her step along the muddy track. Thunder rolled across the hills like distant drums of war.

Through the growing gloom, old stone walls emerged—a chapel forgotten by time but not by grace, its windows dark yet welcoming, its roof still sound against heaven's fury.

"Providence provides," Elara murmured, pushing open the weathered door with a grateful sigh. Ancient hinges creaked their welcome as we stepped inside.

The air tasted of dust and decades of prayers offered to listening ears. Broken pews lined the walls like old soldiers standing vigil, and at the far end, a simple altar waited beneath a window painted with the image of a shepherd gathering scattered sheep.

She laid me carefully beside her bedroll, her fingers lingering on my hilt in the gesture that had become as familiar as breathing. The storm began its fierce dance outside—rain drumming against slate, lightning throwing strange shadows through colored glass that told stories older than memory.

Her breathing deepened into sleep's gentle rhythm, and I settled into my usual watch, content in her peaceful presence, grateful for the shelter and the quiet.

Then shadow moved where no shadow should.

At first I thought it merely wind's mischief, but silent footsteps crossed the chapel floor, carefully avoiding boards that might betray their passage. A figure crept closer through the darkness—eyes fixed not on Elara but on the gleam of my steel.

Thin hands emerged from ragged sleeves, trembling as they reached for me. His touch felt all wrong—cold where Elara's had been warm, desperate where hers had been sure, broken where hers had been beautifully whole.

No! I tried to warn her, to somehow make my voice known, but I remained what I'd always been—steel shaped for purpose but bound by nature's laws. I could only witness as the thief lifted me carefully from beside her sleeping form.

My essence cried out as distance grew between us. Each step took me further from her healing presence, from the purpose I'd found in mercy's bright halls. The thief wrapped me in dirty cloth, muffling my surface as he carried me out into the storm's embrace.

Rain fell against my shrouded form as he hurried through the night. Lightning split the sky like revelation, and in that brief, brilliant moment, I saw something in his face that I recognized—not greed or malice born of evil heart, but desperation deep as dried wells and fear sharp as winter wind.

Perhaps, even now, there were truths to be discovered and choices to be made.

The storm raged on, and I was carried deeper into mystery, wondering if this was how redemption worked—not as straight path from darkness into light, but as winding journey through shadows and sunshine both, each step teaching something the last could not.

In the thief's trembling hands, I felt the echo of my own long pilgrimage toward grace.

5

The Weight of a Hungry Heart

Cold air whispered across my steel as rough hands pulled away the dirty cloth, like curtains opening on a scene I didn't want to witness. Moonlight leaked through a cracked window, painting weak silver across floorboards that had known too many tears.

The thief's touch sent shivers through my essence—so different from Elara's healing warmth, like winter wind after summer sun. My spirit ached at the memory of her gentle hands, at the connection severed by need and night's dark courage.

But as I felt the trembling in those young fingers, as our bond formed the way it always did—reluctant as dawn in deep winter—I discovered something that stopped my anger cold as quenching water.

Such young hands for a thief.

Kieran's presence flooded into my awareness like spilled wine, dark and complex. Barely past childhood, with calluses that spoke of honest work rather than swordplay, and a fresh cut across his palm where he'd caught himself on something sharp during our escape from the chapel.

His thoughts tumbled into mine like scattered coins: guilt warring with necessity, innocence fighting a losing battle against desperation. Through his eyes, I saw what drove him to shadowed choices—three small faces huddled around a cold hearth like birds in a storm.

Amelia with arms too thin wrapped protectively around little *Peter*, while *Lucas* stared hollow-eyed at an empty bowl. The ghost of their parents' absence hung heavy in every corner of their bare home, thick as smoke from a dying fire.

"I'm sorry," he whispered—though whether to me or to some memory of the boy he used to be, I couldn't tell. His conscience weighed on him like wet wool, each theft another stone in the burden he carried. Yet beneath the thief's mask beat a brother's heart, one that would bear any load to see his siblings fed.

The rage I'd expected to feel melted away like frost in spring sun. How could I condemn him when his actions, though crooked as a bent nail, sprang from love pure as well water? I'd witnessed countless battles fought for far lesser reasons—for pride bright as fool's gold, for glory thin as morning mist, for the mere thrill of steel singing its deadly song.

But this boy fought a different kind of war, one waged not with blade and blood but with survival itself, each day another battle against the enemy that hunger makes of hope.

Through our bond, I felt every choice that had led him here—each desperate decision like a wrong turn down a dark path, each compromise of principle another step away from the light, each silent prayer for forgiveness rising like smoke from a guilty heart.

In his struggle, I recognized something of my own journey from weapon of war to instrument of grace. Perhaps we were both learning that sometimes the longest road home begins with admitting you're lost.

* * *

The city's heartbeat pulsed around us as Kieran slipped through narrow passages between buildings that leaned together like old friends sharing secrets. His footsteps fell light as scattered leaves, carrying us deeper into the maze of stone and shadow where desperation made its home.

Moonlight painted silver coins across rain-slicked cobblestones. The night air carried fragments of distant lives—a mother's lullaby drifting from an open window soft as falling snow, the clatter of a late merchant's cart loaded with tomorrow's bread, a cat's yowl echoing off weathered walls like a prayer for warmer days.

Kieran's heart drummed against his ribs with each sound, his grip tightening around my hilt like a lifeline in stormy seas. The weight of his mission pressed down on shoulders too young to bear such loads. Through his eyes, every shadow held potential discovery, every echo threatened exposure.

Yet beneath the fear burned something stronger—an unwavering resolve that blazed like forge-fire in his chest, fed by love that wouldn't let him quit no matter how dark the path became.

We ducked under a broken archway and descended three worn steps to a door that hung crooked on hinges rusty as autumn leaves. Kieran's fingers traced a pattern on the splintered wood—three quick taps, two slow—the secret knock that meant *family* and *home* and *safety*.

The door creaked open just enough to admit a slender body, and then—

"Kier!" A small voice pierced the darkness like sudden sunlight. Tiny arms wrapped around his waist as Peter buried his face in his brother's threadbare coat. "You were gone so long. I was scared the shadows would take you too."

The room beyond held little more than hope and stubborn love. A single candle flickered atop a wooden crate that served as both table and treasure chest—though what treasures these children had were measured not in gold but in the precious fact that they still had each other.

Amelia stirred something in a pot over dying embers, her face too serious for someone who should still believe in fairy tales. Lucas sat cross-legged in the corner, mending a shoe with careful stitches, his concentration fierce as any scholar's over ancient texts.

"Did you get food?" Amelia asked, her voice barely louder than the wind through cracked walls. Her eyes—so like Kieran's, bright with intelligence and shadowed with worry—darted to me hanging at his hip. "What's that?"

"Something better than food," Kieran replied, his voice tight with hope he was trying to make himself believe. "Something that will feed us for months."

I felt the love in his chest—fierce as winter wind, protective as mother bear, absolute as sunrise. In Kieran's heart, I sensed the weight of promises made to parents long gone, the crushing responsibility of being both brother and guardian to souls who depended on him like flowers depend on rain.

Yet here, in this broken place they called home, lived a warmth that no palace could match. Through his eyes, I saw not the peeling walls or patched blankets, but a fortress built from devotion, where each child bore the same quiet strength, the same stubborn refusal to let circumstances break what love had built.

"Where did you get it?" Lucas asked, setting aside his needlework. At thirteen, he was nearly as tall as Kieran, though hunger had carved hollows in his cheeks that spoke of too many meals skipped so the little ones could eat.

"It doesn't matter," Kieran said, ruffling Peter's hair with fingers that trembled slightly. "What matters is what it's worth. What it can buy."

But even as he spoke, I felt his thoughts drift to the shadowy figure he planned to visit—*Silas*, whose very name tasted bitter as wormwood in Kieran's mind. The dealer's reputation lurked in the darker corners of the city like spider's silk—drawing desperate souls into bargains that stained them forever.

I pushed back against these thoughts, letting my essence ripple with warning cold as winter water. Dread seeped through our bond, and Kieran's hand trembled on my hilt. His grip loosened as another memory surfaced—one I hadn't summoned, yet welcomed.

His mother's voice, gentle as candlelight on the last night before the fever took her: "Remember, my brave boy—there's always another choice. When the world grows dark and you can't see the path, look for the light in others. It will show you the way home."

His father's weathered hands, rough from honest work but tender as they smoothed Kieran's hair: "Your mother's right, son. We may not have gold or grand houses, but we have something richer—we know who we are. Don't let hunger or hardship make you forget that. Promise me."

"I promise, Papa."

The memory hit Kieran like a physical blow, and I felt tears sting his eyes as he remembered the boy who'd made that vow with a whole heart. That boy had believed promises were easy to keep, that choosing right was simple as choosing left.

But that boy had never held his sobbing siblings while their stomachs cramped with emptiness. Had never calculated how many days a loaf of bread could stretch, or wondered if the cough in little Peter's chest might be the same fever that claimed their parents.

Still, the memory of their voices—warm as hearthfire, steady as stone—gave him pause. *What would they think of who I've become?* The question whispered through his mind like autumn wind through bare branches.

* * *

The next night smelled of unshed rain, matching the weight in Kieran's chest as he made his way through the city's darker veins. His siblings had asked no questions when he said he'd return with food—they'd learned long ago that hope was fragile as spun glass and twice as likely to shatter.

The streets grew narrower, the buildings leaning closer together like conspirators sharing secrets. Here, in the belly of the city where honest folk feared to tread, deals were struck that daylight never witnessed.

Silas kept his shop in a basement beneath a tavern that had forgotten its own name. The wooden sign above the door hung crooked, its paint peeled away like old scabs. Stone steps led down into darkness that seemed to swallow light rather than simply lacking it.

I felt Kieran's heart hammering against his ribs as he descended. The air grew thick with the smell of unwashed bodies and desperate choices. Lamplight flickered weak as dying hope, casting shadows that danced like demons on damp walls.

"Well, well." The voice oozed from the darkness like oil from a cracked barrel. "Young Kieran returns. What treasures do you bring old Silas today?"

The man who emerged from the shadows looked like hunger given human form—tall, thin as winter branches, with eyes that glittered like coins at the bottom of a well. His smile showed too many teeth, each one sharp as broken promises.

"Something special this time," Kieran managed, his voice steadier than his hands as he unwrapped me from the dirty cloth. "Real quality. Fine steel."

Silas's eyes widened like a cat spotting wounded prey as he examined my surface. His fingers, stained with substances I didn't care to identify, traced Gregory's maker's mark with growing excitement.

"Oh, this is *very* special indeed," he breathed, his voice thick with greed. "Do you know what you've brought me, little sparrow? This is Sir Gregory's work—the greatest smith that ever lived in the three kingdoms. His mark here, see? This blade is worth more than you could imagine."

Kieran's eyes widened. He'd known I was well-made, but the reverence in Silas's voice spoke of value beyond his desperate dreams.

"Sir Gregory died nearly two hundred years ago," Silas continued, his smile spreading like oil on water. "His blades are treasures now, sought by collectors and nobles alike. Where did a street rat like you find such a prize?"

"Does it matter?" Kieran's voice cracked slightly, though now uncertainty crept in alongside the original question. He'd thought he was stealing a good sword—but something this valuable...

"Seventy silver pieces," Silas announced, his voice smooth as snake oil. "More than enough to keep those little birds of yours fed for two winters running."

Something shifted in Kieran's chest. Through our bond, I felt the memory of his parents' voices rising like ghosts from deeper waters:

"We know who we are. Don't let hunger or hardship make you forget that."

I felt his resolve wavering like a candle flame in the wind. This wasn't just theft anymore—this was selling stolen goods to a man who dealt in misery, who would ask no questions because questions might interfere with profit.

The offer hung in the air between them, heavy as storm clouds. I felt Kieran's need warring with his conscience, desperation battling the boy his parents had raised him to be.

"I..." Kieran's voice failed him. He reached for me, his hands trembling, and snatched me. "I can't. I'm sorry, I can't do this."

Silas's friendly mask slipped like badly fitted armor. "Oh, but I think you can, little sparrow. I think you *will*." His smile turned sharp as broken glass. "You see, I know who you are. I know where those precious siblings nest. It would be... unfortunate... if something happened to them while you wrestled with unnecessary conscience."

The threat hit Kieran like a physical blow. I felt fear spike through him, cold as winter iron. But beneath the terror, something else stirred—the same protective fury that had driven him to theft in the first place, now turned toward a worthier target.

"Take the coin," Silas continued, his voice dropping to a whisper that seemed to echo off the damp walls. "Walk away. Forget you ever had doubts. It's simple as breathing."

But Kieran's jaw set like stone. "No." The word came out stronger than he felt. "No, I won't sell what isn't mine to sell."

"You little fool!" Silas snarled, lunging forward. "Do you think you can walk away from me? Do you think I'll let some street rat insult my generosity?"

But Kieran was already moving, desperation lending speed to his feet as he bolted for the stairs. Behind him, Silas shouted orders to unseen associates, his voice echoing like thunder in the narrow space.

Kieran burst onto the street like a cork from a bottle, his breath coming in sharp gasps. Behind him, heavy footsteps pounded up the stone steps. He ran through twisting alleys, taking turns at random, his only thought to put distance between himself and the nightmare he'd nearly embraced.

When he finally stopped, pressing himself against a wall in a narrow passage between two tenements, his whole body shook like leaves in a stormy wind. I felt his terror—not just for himself, but for Amelia, Lucas, and Peter sleeping unaware in their broken home.

"What have I done?" he whispered. "What have I done to them?"

But even as fear clawed at his heart, I felt something else growing stronger—relief, clean as mountain air. He had chosen. When tested, when offered everything he thought he needed, he had chosen to remain the boy his parents raised rather than become the man desperation demanded.

"We have to leave," he murmured. "We have to get them and go. Now."

* * *

The moon was a silver coin tossed against black velvet when Kieran burst through their crooked door, his chest heaving like a blacksmith's bellows. His siblings stirred from sleep on their shared pallet of straw and patched blankets—three small shapes in the darkness lit only by dying embers in their makeshift hearth.

"We have to go," he gasped, already moving toward the corner where they kept their few belongings. "Now. All of us."

"Kier?" Amelia's voice carried the sharp edge of someone jolted from dreams into nightmare. She was sitting up now, her protective instincts flaring even through sleep's fog. "What's happening?"

"I made a mistake," he said, his hands shaking as he stuffed their spare clothes into a canvas sack that had seen better decades. "A bad one. There are men who might come looking, and when they do..." He didn't finish the thought. In the darkness, he didn't need to.

Lucas was awake now too, his thin face grave as winter stone in the ember-light. "How long do we have?"

"Maybe till dawn. Maybe less." Kieran's fingers fumbled for the small jar where they kept their few copper coins—savings that wouldn't buy passage on a merchant's cart but might purchase bread for the road. "Peter, wake up, little brother. We're going on a journey."

The youngest rubbed his eyes with small fists, confusion and trust warring in his sleepy face. "Where are we going?"

"Away from here," Kieran replied, which wasn't really an answer but was all the certainty he possessed. "Can you carry your blanket? We need to travel light and fast."

They moved through the pre-dawn darkness with the desperate efficiency of those who'd practiced leaving in their worst dreams. Everything they owned fit into two sacks and a bundle tied with fraying rope. It wasn't much—but then, you can't lose what you never really had.

The city's streets lay empty except for rats and shadows as they slipped out the back way, avoiding main thoroughfares where Silas's eyes might be watching. Behind them, their broken home stood dark and abandoned—another casualty in the endless war between want and conscience.

They walked through darkness like spirits fleeing the grave, four small figures carrying everything they valued on their backs. The city's edges gave way to countryside that smelled of dew and growing things— honest scents that seemed to wash some of the fear from their lungs.

"There's a village," Kieran said as they followed a road that ribboned pale through rolling hills. "Oakdale, Father called it. Said we had an aunt there—his sister Martha. 'If anything ever happens to us,' he told me once, 'take the little ones to Martha. She'll see you right.'" His voice caught slightly on the memory. "Three days' walk if we keep steady pace. Small enough to disappear in, far enough that Silas's reach won't follow."

Dawn found them huddled in a hayrick beside the road, sharing stale bread and trying to ignore the hollow ache in their bellies. Peter's cough had worsened in the night air—soft, persistent, like autumn leaves refusing to let go of their branches.

"What's she like? Our aunt?" Amelia asked, hope threading through her voice like golden wire through dark cloth.

Kieran's face clouded with uncertainty. "Father didn't speak of her often. Something about a quarrel years ago, before we were born. But blood is blood, he always said. Family helps family when the world grows dark."

Through our bond, I felt his determination burning steady as forge-fire despite the fear that gnawed at his edges. This plan felt fragile as spun glass, built more on hope than certainty, but it was the only thread connecting them to safety.

* * *

Kieran's weariness hung on him like wet wool as we crested the final hill overlooking Oakdale. His muscles ached from carrying Peter when the boy's legs gave out, and worry gnawed at his thoughts as we wandered streets that felt both welcoming and foreign.

The village spread across the valley like a quilt thrown over sleeping earth—smoke rising from chimneys against the afternoon sky, fields of wheat ripening gold as scattered coins. A water wheel turned lazy circles at the settlement's edge, keeping time with the rhythm of simple life. After three days on the road, sleeping in ditches and eating berries that tasted of hope and desperation, the sight of civilization brought tears to Amelia's eyes bright as morning dew.

Each inquiry about Aunt Martha led to blank stares or shaken heads—kindly enough, but final as closed doors. The children's spirits dimmed with each disappointment, their hopes washing away like chalk drawings in rain.

An old man sat outside the village bakery, his weathered hands whittling wood. The knife's rhythmic scraping paused as Kieran approached, courage and fear wrestling in his chest.

"Excuse me, sir. I'm looking for Martha Bennett?"

The man's face creased with thought, his knife hovering over the half-formed bird taking shape in his palms. "Martha? Oh, child." The words carried the gentle weight of sorrows shared. "Poor soul passed in her sleep three winters ago. Peaceful as candles guttering out, the midwife said."

Kieran's grip tightened on my hilt, despair seeping through our bond like cold water through cracked stone. Lucas kicked at the dirt with the frustrated energy of someone who'd carried hope too far only to watch it crumble. Amelia pulled Peter closer to her side, her arms forming a shelter against disappointment.

The man must have noticed the way their faces fell, for he added quickly, "Her cottage still stands, though, out past the miller's wheel, where the oak grove begins. A woman lives there now, though she does travel often. She could be related."

"Thank you," Kieran managed, his voice thick as honey mixed with tears.

We found the cottage as the sun dipped toward the horizon like a golden coin slipping into a purse. Ivy claimed one wall with the patient persistence of time itself, and tall grass swayed around the stone foundation like dancers to unheard music. Through windows that had forgotten their glass, dust motes spun lazy pirouettes in the dying light.

The door hung askew on hinges brown as autumn rust, creaking soft lullabies to the evening breeze.

"Home sweet home," Lucas muttered, his attempt at humor.

"It's better than nothing," Kieran replied. "At least we have a roof over our heads and walls to keep the wind at bay."

But as we crossed that crooked threshold, warmth spilled out to meet us—not the cold emptiness of abandonment, but the golden glow of candlelight and the scent of herbs that spoke of care and healing.

My essence surged with recognition like a bell struck true. *That gentle presence. That familiar warmth.*

Elara.

She stood by a worn table that had known countless meals and whispered conversations, grinding herbs. Her silver-streaked hair caught the firelight.

I felt Kieran's heart seize with shock sharp as winter wind. His fingers trembled against my hilt as understanding crashed over him like a wave against an unsuspecting shore. The sword he'd stolen, the woman he'd wronged—and here, in this impossible moment, their paths crossing again like threads in some vast tapestry he couldn't see the pattern of.

"I... I..." The words stuck in his throat like burrs on wool.

His siblings huddled behind him, confusion written across their young faces. With hands that shook like leaves in a stormy wind, he unclasped me from his belt and knelt, presenting me across his palms like an offering on some ancient altar.

"This belongs to you," he whispered, his voice breaking like ice in spring thaw. "I'm the one who stole it."

The confession poured out then—tales of empty cupboards that echoed like hollow drums, of hungry cries that pierced long nights, of choices made with hearts heavy as lead and consciences twisted like rope under strain. Through our bond, I felt his shame burning bright as forge-fire, hot enough to melt steel.

"I didn't know you'd be here," he finished, tears cutting clean tracks down cheeks dirty from the road. "I thought the cottage was empty."

Elara's steps whispered across floorboards worn smooth by Martha's faithful feet. Her familiar touch brushed my pommel—gentle as benediction, warm as hearthlight—and joy sang through my steel like bells calling the faithful home.

But her eyes remained fixed on Kieran's bowed head, taking in the weight he carried, the love that had driven him to dark choices, the courage it took to confess when he could have simply fled.

"Look at me, child," she said gently—the tone that could calm storms in troubled hearts.

Kieran raised his face, tear-stained and expecting judgment, but finding instead compassion warm as summer rain in her gaze.

"I see no thief before me," Elara said, her words settling over the frightened family like blankets against a cold night. "Only a brother trying to protect what matters most." She gestured to the hungry faces peering from behind him. "Come, all of you. The stew is almost ready, and I have fresh bread cooling on the windowsill—enough to fill bellies that have been empty far too long."

Relief and gratitude flooded through Kieran like spring water through drought-cracked ground as Elara lifted me from his trembling hands. "But... how can you forgive so easily? How can you welcome someone who wronged you?"

"Because I understand what love drives us to do," she replied, setting me gently against the wall with the reverence of someone placing a sleeping child in its cradle. "And because the best cure for a thief is to give him reason not to steal." She turned to her herb-laden shelves, hands already reaching for what Peter's cough would need. "Now, let's tend that illness your youngest brother is trying to hide, and then we'll talk about properly feeding growing children."

Peter stepped forward shyly, wonder bright in his eyes. "How did you know I was coughing?"

Elara's smile deepened the lines around her eyes. "A healer learns to see what mere eyes cannot. Just as I knew Truthseeker would find his way back to me—though I didn't expect him to bring such precious company."

Over bowls of stew thick as kindness and twice as nourishing, Elara spoke of possibilities that took root in young hearts like seeds in fertile ground. Her words carried the healing power I'd witnessed countless times—mending wounds that went deeper than flesh, binding up what life had torn.

The children's faces, pinched with hunger and worry for so long they'd forgotten what contentment looked like, gradually softened in the warm glow of both fire and hope.

"Master Willem's workshop lies just beyond the grain mill," Elara said, ladling more stew into Peter's bowl until abundance threatened to spill over its rim. "Fine craftsman, that one—works with wood and stone and honest metal. His hands aren't as steady as they once were, and he needs someone quick to learn and careful with detail work."

Kieran's fingers traced absent patterns on the wooden table, as if trying to carve better futures from worn grain. "I... I've always been good with my hands. Father taught me carpentry before the fever took him. Said I had the feel for it."

"Then perhaps that's no mere chance." Elara's eyes held the knowing gleam of someone who saw threads connecting where others saw only coincidence. "Skills given freely become gifts that can be shared—used to build rather than break, to create rather than take."

I felt hope kindle in Kieran's heart like tinder catching spark. Images bloomed in his mind—not of shadowed alleys and desperate theft, but of honest work done in honest light, hands that built beauty rather than stealing it, siblings who could grow up proud of their brother's trade.

"And you, dear heart," Elara continued, turning to Amelia with the gentle attention, "have the careful touch needed for herb work. I could use an apprentice—someone with steady hands and a kind spirit."

Amelia's eyes brightened like stars emerging from behind clouds. "You would teach me? About healing?"

"About healing, yes. And growing, and mixing, and seeing what troubles people before they know it themselves. It's good work—the kind that feeds the soul as much as the coin-purse."

Lucas looked up from his bowl, hope and uncertainty dancing in his expression like flames in the wind. "What about me?"

"Strong arms are always welcome at Henrik's mill," Elara replied without pause. "And little ones," she added, ruffling Peter's hair until giggles spilled out like coins from a torn purse, "are excellent at gathering eggs from cranky hens—too quick for the birds to peck."

Watching this transformation, I felt something profound shift within my own essence, like metal cooling into its truest shape. How many times had I dwelt on lives taken through my edge, blood spilled by pride and hatred's sharp hunger? Yet here, witnessing Kieran's choice to walk from shadow toward light, I grasped something deep about the nature of grace.

If Elara could look past theft to see the love that drove it, if this boy could choose better paths despite the weight of desperate choices, perhaps I too, could release the burden of former deeds that clung to my steel like rust.

The prideful warrior's actions had been his own choosing, his fall a path he'd walked with eyes wide open. My purpose wasn't carved by how others had wielded me, but by the truth I helped reveal—in them, and finally, perhaps, in myself.

Like Kieran, I could choose what I would become.

A memory stirred in my steel then—clear as spring water, warm as Gregory's forge on the day he first breathed consciousness into my metal heart:

"You were made to guard, not to take. To kindle hope, not to snuff it out."

His words rang through my essence now, watching Kieran's transformation unfold like flowers opening to the sun. I hadn't simply exposed his theft—I'd helped him uncover the truth of his own heart, the nobility that hardship had buried but never quite managed to kill.

The final piece of memory settled into place like a key finding a lock: *"You are Truthseeker. For that's your gift—helping folk find their way to what's real and right and true."*

As the children settled into sleep around the hearth—bellies full for the first time in memory, faces peaceful as evening prayer—Elara lifted me from my place against the wall. Her familiar touch welcomed me like sunrise after long darkness.

She carried me outside where moonlight painted her herb garden in silver, catching on my surface like captured starshine. Night-blooming jasmine sweetened the air while somewhere in the darkness an owl asked questions of the listening world.

"You've learned much in our time apart," she whispered, fingers tracing Gregory's mark with reverence usually reserved for sacred texts. "As have I. Perhaps we were meant to find these children—you through your journey into shadow, I through mine toward deeper understanding."

I felt her gentle wisdom, her unshakable faith that everything—even separation and theft, even pain and desperate midnight choices—served purposes larger than the moment could contain.

"Tomorrow brings fresh beginnings," she said, gazing at stars that had witnessed countless such moments throughout the turning years. "For all of us."

Her words settled into my essence like a blessing, offering comfort while stirring questions that rustled within me like leaves in a gentle wind. I had glimpsed fragments of understanding—that my purpose involved revealing truth rather than simply dealing death, helping souls find their way rather than cutting through obstacles.

But mysteries remained, deep as ancient wells and twice as dark. Why had Gregory chosen to gift mere steel with awareness? What calling could justify the weight of consciousness, the burden of witnessing both cruelty and kindness through countless hands?

Each wielder had taught me something different about hearts that beat in mortal chests—the warrior's pride, Elara's compassion, Kieran's desperate love. Yet still my own truth remained elusive as a horizon that retreats with every step taken toward it.

Perhaps, I thought as Elara carried me back inside to stand guard over sleeping grace, my purpose wasn't destination but journey. Perhaps Gregory had awakened me not to solve some grand mystery, but to gather wisdom through connection, to grow in understanding even as I helped others find paths through shadow toward light.

The question of *why* might never find its answer. But watching over the children—faces peaceful despite all they'd endured—I felt deep rightness in this moment, this place, this choice to guard love's small victories.

Whatever ultimate calling might await, tonight I had helped guide lost souls toward healing. And perhaps, when all accounts were settled, that would prove sufficient.

After all, the most precious truths often hide in plain sight, dressed as ordinary mercy.

6

The Heart That Knew Its Calling

The years had worn the sharp edges off my grief like river stones smoothed by patient water. My last memory of Elara and Kieran remained bright as polished copper—her white hair catching sunset like spun silver as she pressed me into his weathered hands. His own children played in the workshop yard beyond, their laughter mixing with the ring of hammer on honest metal, sweet as church bells on Sunday morning.

"Keep him safe," she'd whispered, her healing touch brushing my pommel one final time like benediction. "Let him guide others as he guided you toward light."

Kieran had promised to find me a worthy bearer, someone who would understand the weight of purpose that rode heavier than any blade. The path that led me to this dusty armory in Veladorn twisted through many hands—some gentle, some rough, all teaching me fragments of the great mystery that was the human heart. Yet I held fast to the truth I'd learned from them both: my power lay not in dealing death like a reaper's scythe, but in revealing light hidden beneath the surface of things.

Still, questions lingered in my steel. Why had Gregory gifted mere metal with awareness? What calling could justify the burden of consciousness in something forged for battle? I had glimpsed pieces of understanding through each bearer's hands, yet the complete picture remained elusive as morning mist.

Dust motes danced in the thin shaft of sunlight piercing the armory's gloom, lazy as summer flies. My thoughts scattered like startled sparrows at the echo of footsteps approaching down the stone corridor—purposeful steps that spoke of someone who knew their mind.

The wooden door creaked open on hinges that remembered better days, torchlight spilling across rows of lesser blades like golden honey over fresh bread.

"Here, Sir Edmund." A young voice rang with barely contained excitement. "I found it while organizing the back racks. See how the steel catches the light? I've never seen markings quite like these."

The torchlight drew closer, and I felt the presence of two souls—one young and eager as spring sap, the other steady and resolute as oak roots grown deep. The knight's footsteps fell with the measured cadence of someone accustomed to bearing weight beyond his years.

"Indeed, Thomas." Sir Edmund's voice carried warmth and wisdom in equal measure, like bread fresh from the oven and tea steeped to perfection. "I've heard tales of such craftsmanship. Bring that torch closer, lad."

Young Thomas lifted his light higher, and I felt Edmund's gaze travel along my length like a careful examination of fine workmanship. His spirit touched mine in that first contact, and through that brief connection, I sensed something that made my steel sing with recognition—an echo of the same noble heart that had first shaped me in Gregory's forge.

Sir Edmund's calloused fingers traced the maker's mark near my hilt with the reverence usually reserved for sacred things, and his breath caught sharp as winter air. "By all the stars in heaven... Thomas, do you know what this is?"

The squire leaned closer, torch flame wavering. "No, my lord. Just that it's finer than anything else in this forgotten place."

"This is Truthseeker—Sir Gregory's final masterpiece." Edmund's voice filled with the kind of reverence monks reserved for holy relics. "Such balance, such grace in every line. The stories you must hold, old friend... How does a blade of this caliber end up forgotten in a castle's dusty corners?"

His touch resonated through my being like a struck bell calling faithful to prayer, awakening memories of the forge where I drew first breath. The same nobility of spirit that had guided Gregory's hammer now flowed through Edmund's weathered hands. Here was a soul who understood duty not as a burden to be borne, but as a sacred trust to be cherished.

(Now, you might wonder how steel recognizes kindred spirits, but honor calls to honor across any distance, like iron filings drawn to a lodestone—some attractions run deeper than the eye can see.)

"The king did say you could choose anything you wished from the armory, Sir Edmund." Thomas shifted from foot to foot like a child with good news bursting to be shared. "For your service in the northern campaign against those brigands threatening the merchant roads."

My connection deepened with Edmund as his fingers found their proper place around my hilt. His thoughts echoed with visions clear— defending village folk from raiders, standing between the weak and those who would devour them like wolves among sheep. This was a knight who saw his strength as a shield for others, not as a sword for personal glory.

"Yes." Edmund's grip settled around my handle with the rightness of a key finding a lock. "With this blade, I will protect those who cannot protect themselves. It seems fitting that Truthseeker should serve such a purpose—Sir Gregory once wrote that a sword's highest calling was to preserve life, not harvest it."

The conviction in his voice stirred something deep in my essence, like distant thunder promising rain to drought-parched ground. Here was a wielder who might truly grasp what my creator intended, who could help me fulfill the purpose for which I was forged in fire and hope.

* * *

Through Edmund's steady grip, I felt the weight of ceremony as we entered the throne room. Sunlight streamed through tall windows painted with kings and stories, casting the marble floor in jeweled hues that shifted like living water. King Leofric sat upon his throne carved from ancient oak, his crown catching afternoon light like captured sunshine. At his right hand stood Prince Zevrin, shadows playing across his features despite the room's brightness—or perhaps because of something darker that lived within.

"Edmund, my boy!" King Leofric's voice filled the chamber with warmth that could thaw winter's deepest freeze. His eyes fell to where I hung at Edmund's side, and interest sparked in their depths like flint striking steel. "What's this? A new blade to grace your hip?"

Edmund drew me with fluid grace that spoke of years spent learning steel's proper dance, presenting me flat across his palms like an offering. "Your Majesty, fate has smiled upon me with unexpected generosity. This is Truthseeker, Sir Gregory's masterwork."

"Truthseeker?" The king rose from his throne, each step down the marble stairs measured and deliberate. Through Edmund's touch, I sensed the genuine affection between these two men—not merely king and knight bound by duty's chains, but something warmer, closer to father and son. "To think such a legendary blade would find its way to you. There could be no worthier bearer in all the realm."

A sharp laugh cut through the moment like broken glass against silk.

"Worthy? A common knight bearing such a weapon?" Prince Zevrin's words dripped venom sweet as poisoned honey as he lounged against the throne's arm, fingers drumming against polished wood with restless malice. "Perhaps it's merely clever imitation, like its wielder's pretense at true nobility."

The temperature in the room seemed to drop. King Leofric turned slowly to face his son, disappointment etched in every line of his weathered face. "You forget yourself, Zevrin. Sir Edmund has proven his worth a hundred times over, each deed worth more than idle words. You will apologize for this discourtesy. Now."

Zevrin's jaw clenched tight as a miser's purse, and through Edmund's grip I felt the prince's spirit twist with dark emotions—jealousy coiled around his heart like a serpent around a dove's nest, squeezing out all light and leaving only bitter shadow.

"I... apologize for my hasty words, Sir Edmund." The words fell from his lips like coins grudgingly paid. "If you'll excuse me, Father, I have other matters requiring my attention."

The prince's boots clicked against marble with sharp staccato rhythm as he strode from the chamber, yet his shadow seemed to linger even after he'd gone—a cold presence that made honest souls shiver without knowing why.

King Leofric's genuine remorse radiated across the chamber like heat from banked coals. "Edmund, forgive my son's outburst. His words bring shame to crown and kingdom both."

"Your Majesty shows too much kindness. No apology needed." Edmund's voice held no resentment. Through our bond, I felt his pity for the prince—not scorn, but sorrow for a soul so twisted by envy it could no longer see light.

The king's weathered fingers traced the engravings along my blade with a touch as gentle as a grandmother's blessing. "We have pressing concerns that require immediate attention. News arrived this morning from Casterbridge, near the Malvorian border."

Edmund's grip tightened ever so slightly. "The bridge town that guards the river crossing?"

"The same. Raiders strike without warning, yet our stationed knights fail to stop them. Three attacks in the past month alone, each one growing bolder." The king's voice dropped to a tone reserved for the gravest matters. "Something feels wrong about this, Edmund. The timing, the precision... I fear more than simple banditry at work."

"You suspect treachery, Your Majesty?"

"I trust my instincts as I trust you—completely." King Leofric squared shoulders that had borne the crown's weight through two decades of rule. "Take whatever men you need. Find the truth behind these raids before more innocent blood waters our soil."

Edmund's bow was as graceful as a swan on a still pond, his spirit resonating with determination as solid as mountain stone. "I'll depart at first light, Sire."

"The kingdom of Valandria owes you a debt beyond payment, Sir Edmund." The king clasped Edmund's shoulder with a hand that trembled slightly—not from weakness, but from emotion held in check. "Your service honors us all."

* * *

I felt the evening air grow thick with menace as we turned down the narrow alley, like storm clouds gathering overhead. Shadows stretched like grasping fingers across cobblestones worn smooth by countless feet, and something in the unnatural stillness made my steel sing with warning.

"Draw your blade, Thomas," Edmund commanded, his voice low but steady. "Stay close and watch the rooftops."

The whisper of steel leaving leather filled the air as Edmund drew me from my scabbard. In that moment, dark figures materialized from doorways and shadowed corners like nightmare creatures stepping from bad dreams into the waking world.

The first attacker lunged with deadly intent, his blade arcing toward Edmund's throat like a striking serpent. Edmund's parry flowed like water over stone, my edge catching moonlight as we deflected the strike. I felt his focus sharpen—not on glory or dominance that fed pride's hungry maw, but on protecting the young squire at his back.

Steel rang against steel with the voice of honest conflict as Thomas fought beside us, his training showing in each defensive move. Edmund's swordwork remained precise, each strike measured and necessary. No wasted motion, no flourish for vanity's sake—just clean efficiency born of righteous purpose.

A blade whistled past Edmund's guard like an angry wasp, slicing through his sleeve to draw first blood. We pivoted smooth as dancers, and in one fluid motion, my edge found flesh. The attacker crumpled to cobblestones, his blood staining ancient stones darker than night.

Ice shot through my essence like winter wind through a cracked shutter. *Blood. Death.* The old familiar taste of mortality, bitter on my steel. But this felt different from the warrior's savage joy in killing, different as honey from gall. Through Edmund's heart, I felt sorrow for life's necessity mixed with unwavering resolve to protect his charge.

This wasn't murder born of pride or hatred's poison. This was the heavy burden of defending innocent light against encroaching darkness. Still, the weight of taking life settled into my steel like shadow at sunset. How many more would fall before my edge? Even in a righteous cause, death left its mark on both blade and soul.

Yet Edmund's spirit remained steady as the North Star, his purpose clear—not to destroy for destruction's sake, but to preserve what was precious and good. Perhaps this too was part of my calling—not just to reveal truth hidden in hearts, but to defend it when revelation wasn't enough.

I felt Edmund's heartbeat slow like spent bellows as the last attacker melted into shadows. Blood dripped from my blade, each crimson drop a testament to the grim work required of those who stand between light and darkness.

"Are you hurt, Thomas?" Edmund's eyes scanned his squire for injuries with care a father might show a beloved son.

"No, sir. Just scratches that will heal quick enough." Thomas wiped sweat from his brow with a trembling hand, his young face pale as parchment in moonlight. "Common thieves, do you think?"

Edmund knelt beside one of the fallen, fingers brushing the quality leather of the man's boots with practiced assessment. "These men were too well-equipped for simple brigands seeking easy coin."

I sensed his growing unease as he examined their gear like a scholar reading an ancient text. The fallen attackers wore no insignias to mark their loyalty, but their weapons told a different tale entirely. Finely crafted swords lay scattered across cobblestones, their edges honed by expert hands that knew steel's secrets.

"Look at their blades, Thomas." Edmund lifted one of the swords, testing its balance with a knowing touch. "Perfect weight distribution. Master craftsmanship throughout. These are soldiers' weapons, not cutthroats' rough tools."

I felt Edmund's mind working through implications like puzzle pieces falling into place. Professional soldiers or hired swords operating in the shadows of Valandria's very capital. But to what dark end?

"Something deeper lies behind this attack than simple robbery." Edmund sheathed me with careful precision. "But without prisoners to question or markings to trace…"

His thoughts turned to our upcoming mission like a compass needle finding true north. Could there be a connection between these shadow-warriors and the troubles plaguing Casterbridge? The timing seemed too convenient for mere coincidence, yet without proof, such suspicions remained just that—suspicions floating groundless as dandelion seeds on the wind.

* * *

The soft scrape of whetstone against my edge filled the quiet chamber like gentle rain on roof tiles as Edmund worked by candlelight. His touch was different from others who had wielded me through the years—reverent yet familiar, like greeting an old friend returned from a distant journey.

Through our deepening connection, I felt his appreciation for craftsmanship and care that went beyond mere maintenance into the realm of sacred ritual.

"You know," Edmund spoke softly as he applied oil to my blade with a cloth worn smooth by countless such evenings, "my father taught me to respect the sword as more than mere steel and leather. 'A blade is your partner in all things,' he'd say. 'Treat it with honor and it will never fail you when failure means death.'"

His hands paused in their work, memories washing through our bond like tide bringing treasures to shore. "He was captain of the village guard in a small town much like Casterbridge will prove to be. Taught me everything worthwhile about honor, about standing firm when darkness comes calling, about protecting those who cannot protect themselves."

Edmund's voice grew thick with emotion held in check as he began polishing my surface. "Raiders came one night when the autumn moon was dark and hope seemed a distant thing. Father stood alone at the village gate while townspeople fled through secret paths. He...He bought them precious time with coin of his own life's blood."

I felt the raw ache of that loss, still fresh as an open wound after so many turning years. But beneath pain lay something stronger—resolve unshakable as mountain bedrock.

"I made a promise at his grave that cold morning when the earth took him back. That I would continue his work, be a shield for those who have none, and stand guard where he could stand no longer. It's not about glory bright as fool's gold or recognition from those who never soil their hands with honest work. It's about doing what's right, even when no one watches, even when a righteous path leads through shadow and suffering."

As he spoke these words with conviction, something profound shifted between us. His truth resonated through my very essence, awakening echoes of Gregory's original purpose in shaping me. This was what I was meant for—not to serve pride's empty hunger or power's cruel ambition, but to aid those who stood in defense of justice and light against encroaching darkness.

"Strange," Edmund murmured, holding me up to candlelight that painted us both in golden hues. "I feel as though you understand these words, as if you were forged for precisely this calling."

In that moment, our spirits aligned, perfectly fitted, joining in a master carpenter's work—guardian and blade, protector and tool, united in purpose that transcended mere metal and flesh. Through Edmund, I glimpsed another piece of my mysterious calling, another fragment of the great puzzle that was my existence.

Yet still I wondered—was this the culmination of my long journey, or merely another step toward some greater understanding that waited patiently at dawn for its appointed hour?

* * *

I watched as our horses emerged from the dense forest into a clearing atop wind-swept cliffs. The autumn air carried the sound of weeping before we saw its source—a hillside dotted with fresh graves like a terrible crop, the earth still dark and raw as open wounds.

Edmund's heart clenched like a fist around a burning coal, the pain flowing through our bond as we witnessed a young girl laying wildflowers on a mound of earth no longer than she was tall. Nearby, a father held two small children while another grave received its final blessing, their mother's last rest marked only by a rough wooden cross and love too deep for words.

The raw grief carved in their faces cut deeper than any blade could reach—honest sorrow that spoke of lives stolen by violence, of children who would grow up with empty places at their table where laughter used to live.

"My lord..." Edmund's squire whispered, his voice breaking.

Edmund's grip tightened on my hilt, his knuckles white as fresh snow with restrained emotion. Protective fury tempered by deep sorrow surged through him like a river in flood time. This wasn't the clean death of soldiers choosing their fate on a field of honor—this was the savage destruction of innocent lives, brutal as a wolf in a chicken coop.

As we descended into the town proper, the devastation grew more apparent with each step. Blackened timbers reached toward the sky like accusing fingers pointing at heaven's apparent silence. Market stalls lay splintered and broken, their goods scattered and ruined like hopes after a storm's passing. A child's doll lay face down in the mud, one arm missing, abandoned in what must have been a frantic flight toward uncertain safety.

Through Edmund's keen eyes, I noted details that spoke of the raiders' calculated brutality. Door hinges torn free with deliberate force. Scorch marks showing purposeful patterns of burning. This was no simple banditry seeking easy profit.

Edmund dismounted near the town square, his boots crunching on broken glass from the tavern's shattered windows. An old woman swept debris from her doorstep, as if trying to brush away more than just the physical remnants of violence.

"How many attacks have you suffered?" Edmund asked her gently.

"Four." Her voice was hollow as an empty grain barrel, her eyes fixed on the task that gave purpose to hands that shook with more than age. "Each time they take more than just goods and coin. Each time they leave us with fresh graves to dig and children who wake screaming in the night."

At the town's center square, I beheld the chapel's weathered stone walls now serving as a makeshift place of healing. Rows of wounded townspeople lay on pallets stuffed with straw, their groans echoing off the sacred walls like prayers too broken for proper words. The scent of blood and herbal poultices hung thick as incense in the air heavy with suffering.

"Help them," Edmund commanded his men, who immediately moved to assist the overwhelmed priest and villagers struggling to tend so many hurts with so few hands.

Edmund knelt beside a young man with a deep gash across his shoulder, and I felt the steady confidence in his hands as he began cleaning the wound with skill born of battlefield experience. The priest—Father James by name—worked alongside him, his worn robes stained with evidence of endless hours spent binding wounds and offering what comfort words could provide.

"Where are the knights who were stationed here?" Edmund asked while pressing a clean bandage to the wound with gentle pressure. "Surely they didn't abandon their post?"

Father James's hands stilled for a moment that stretched like a held breath. "They left us to face the darkness alone. Two days before the first attack, they simply... vanished like morning mist. No word, no warning, no explanation." His voice carried the weight of betrayal, sharp as broken glass. "The keep has stood empty and silent since that day."

I sensed Edmund's shock ripple into controlled anger that burned clean as forge fire. "They abandoned their sacred duty? Left innocent people defenseless before wolves?"

"Some say they were bought with gold." The priest's words came out barely above a whisper, as if speaking louder might make the terrible truth more real. "Others believe they were threatened with something worse than death. All we know for certain is that we were left to stand alone against enemies who show no mercy to the helpless."

A woman nearby sobbed as her wounds were tended, the sound cutting through the chapel's somber atmosphere. "We've lost so many," she wept. "Our children... our homes... everything we built with honest work."

Edmund's heart constricted at her words like a rope around his chest, yet his hands never faltered as he continued ministering to the wounded. The hopelessness pressing against the chapel walls felt thick as smoke— these people had been betrayed by those sworn to protect them, left to face brutality alone when they most needed defending hands.

But in Edmund's touch, in his presence among them, I felt something else beginning to kindle—not false hope built on empty promises, but real possibility that someone still remembered what oaths meant, what duty looked like when lived rather than merely spoken.

* * *

The harsh blare of war horns shattered the morning silence like a hammer on an anvil. I felt Edmund's muscles tense like a bowstring drawn taut as he spotted dark shapes emerging from the tree line on the far bank.

"To arms!" Edmund's voice rang clear and strong. "Form ranks! Archers to the belfries where height gives advantage!"

His men moved with precision born of countless drills, their shields interlocking like scales on a dragon's back as they took defensive positions. The townspeople who could still fight grabbed whatever weapons they possessed—pitchforks, axes, and ancient family blades passed down through generations.

Edmund raised me high so the sunlight caught my steel, a bright beacon against the gathering storm. "For Valandria! For justice! For those who cannot defend themselves!"

The enemy crashed against our lines like a dark wave against a stubborn shore. Through Edmund's skilled hands, I danced through the battle—not with the prideful fury that once consumed my essence, but with righteous purpose clean as mountain water. Each strike defended an innocent life, each parry prevented another orphan or widow from joining sorrow's endless ranks.

Steel rang against steel with an honest voice as Edmund led the charge across the bridge worn smooth by peaceful feet. His tactical mind guided our movements like a master musician conducting a symphony of war, pressing advantages where the enemy showed weakness, supporting where our line grew thin.

I felt his unwavering focus, his determination to protect those who couldn't protect themselves from predators wearing human form. This was what heroism looked like when stripped of grand tales and golden songs—simply standing firm when others would flee, holding the line when hope grew thin.

The battle turned when Edmund's flanking maneuver caught the attackers by surprise, their confidence crumbling like a poorly built wall. Their ordered lines broke into panicked retreat as they fled back across the river toward the forest that had spawned them, leaving their dead to feed the carrion birds.

The sight of enemy backs disappearing into the tree line brought cheers from the townspeople that rang sweet as a harvest festival, voices raised in celebration of life preserved against terrible odds.

"We've shown them our strength," Edmund declared, wiping my blade clean. "But knowledge is a weapon sharper than any steel. We must learn where they hide, how many they number, what master pays their bloody wages."

"Marcus," he called to one of his most trusted men—a grizzled veteran whose scars told stories of a dozen campaigns. "Take two riders and scout their trail like hunting hounds. I want to know their numbers, their camp's location, their supply lines—everything that might give us an advantage in the next encounter."

As Marcus rode out with his chosen companions, I witnessed hope rekindling in the townspeople's eyes like banked coals stirring to life. Children peeked out from hiding places where they'd waited through terror, women emerged from the chapel's protective walls, and men stood straighter, pride returning to bearing that had been bent by fear and loss.

A couple of days passed before Marcus returned, his face grim as a winter storm as he delivered his report. These were no common brigands seeking easy plunder—their encampment bore the disciplined layout of Malvorian military forces, their weapons and armor marked with the kingdom's serpent insignia that spoke of official sanction rather than a rogue operation.

Edmund's pulse quickened like a drumbeat calling soldiers to war as he penned an urgent message to King Leofric. The implications weighed heavy as an anvil in his heart—this was no mere border raid seeking easy spoils, but the opening movement in a larger symphony of invasion.

But as the messenger spurred his horse toward the capital's distant walls, the war horns' cry split the dawn like an axe through seasoned wood. I felt Edmund's battle focus sharpen to a point keen as a needle as he drew me from my scabbard.

The Malvorian forces struck hard as a mountain avalanche, their trained soldiers pressing our defenses with coordination that spoke of professional command. Officers shouted orders while formations moved like pieces on a warboard.

We met them at the bridge's center where stone had witnessed a thousand peaceful crossings, Edmund's bladework precise as a master craftsman's tool. Each strike I delivered felt clean and necessary—protecting these innocent lives from those who would extinguish them like snuffing candles. Yet the cost proved dear as a dragon's hoard. I felt Edmund's grief spike sharp as a broken bone each time one of his men fell, their sacrifice buying precious moments for the townspeople to reach sanctuary.

As the last enemy retreated across the river like beaten dogs slinking home, a rider galloped in from the southern road, his horse white with lather and his eyes wild with urgency. "My lord! A force of two thousand crosses the southern pass like an army of ants! They'll be here within three days' hard march!"

Edmund's mind raced through calculations—our depleted numbers, the town's vulnerable position caught between hammer and anvil, the impossibility of holding against attacks from two directions at once. His decision crystallized with clarity

"We must evacuate before the trap closes tight," Edmund announced to the gathered townspeople. "Pack only what you can carry on your backs. You leave for the northern territories before dawn lights the eastern sky."

The weight of leadership settled over him like a heavy cloak as he watched families prepare to abandon homes and livelihoods built through generations of honest sweat. Yet I felt his certainty—better to lose buildings that could be rebuilt than lives that could never be recovered.

* * *

We watched the townspeople gather their meager possessions like refugees from a terrible dream. The wounded moaned from their pallets in the chapel where Father James moved among them like a shepherd tending an injured flock, while the elderly and sick huddled together, too frail to attempt the journey through the wilderness toward uncertain safety.

"My lord, I should stay by your side," Thomas pleaded, his young face bearing the marks of recent battle—a fresh cut above his eye still crusted with dried blood, a bruise darkening his cheek. "My place is with you wherever the path may lead."

Edmund's hand rested firm on my hilt as he faced his squire. "The people need protection on their journey more than I need company in mine. Half our remaining men will go with you to guard their passage."

"But sir—"

"There are those who cannot travel," Edmund cut in, his voice gentle but brooking no argument like a father explaining harsh necessities to a beloved child. "The wounded, the sick, the elderly who would die on the road before reaching safety. They need defenders here more than I need sword-brothers."

I sensed Edmund's deep conviction flowing like an underground spring. Each labored breath from the chapel, each pained whimper, each tearful goodbye strengthened his resolve to stand guard over those who could not flee when wisdom counseled flight.

"Return with reinforcements," Edmund clasped Thomas's shoulder with a grip that conveyed more than words. "Show these people the same protection I would give them with my own hands. That is your duty now, lad. That is your calling."

Thomas's eyes glistened with tears, but he straightened his spine and nodded with dignity beyond his years. "I will not fail you, sir. Not in this or anything else you ask."

"You never have," Edmund replied softly.

I felt Edmund's heart swell with paternal affection as he watched Thomas organize the evacuation with skill that would have made a seasoned captain proud—directing people into groups, ensuring the strongest helped the weakest. The young squire had grown from an uncertain boy into a capable leader, and now he would prove himself further on the road ahead.

The pre-dawn darkness swallowed the long line of refugees like a gentle mouth accepting an offered meal as they began their journey eastward toward hope and safety. Thomas rode at their head with his shoulders squared by newfound responsibility.

Edmund stood watching until the last flickering light disappeared beyond the hill's crest, then turned back to those who remained with his grip tightening around my hilt—his expression set with grim determination that would have moved mountains if mountains could be moved by will alone.

Those who stayed behind were his to protect now. His to guard. His to die for if darkness demanded such payment for their safety.

And I knew, with certainty that rang through my steel, that he would pay whatever price was asked.

Edmund's weariness seeped into my steel as we gazed across the bridge through morning mist that rose from the water like spirits seeking heaven. Three days had passed since we'd bought precious time for the townspeople to flee—three days of holding the narrow crossing against waves of relentless attacks that broke against our determination like tides against an unyielding cliff.

Though his voice remained steady and his stance proud as a banner in the wind, I felt the bone-deep exhaustion that plagued him like a fever. His remaining men saw only their commander's unwavering resolve, but I knew every ache, every strain, every moment of fatigue he bore in silence for their sake.

The sound of hoof beats pulled Edmund's attention from the bridge where shadows stirred with the promise of violence. We saw Thomas riding hard from the north, his horse's flanks lathered with sweat.

"My lord!" Thomas reined in before us, his chest heaving like bellows worked too hard. "The King's army marches! Six hours at most before they arrive!"

Relief flooded through our bond like spring water after drought, but Edmund's tactical mind never ceased its careful calculations. His gaze swept back to the bridge where enemy movements stirred in the morning shadows like predators scenting weakness.

"They won't wait that long," Edmund's voice carried across his gathered men. "They'll strike before help arrives, hoping to finish what they started before reinforcements can spoil their feast."

He drew me from my scabbard, and I felt the weight of command settle over him like a mantle passed down through generations as he addressed his remaining warriors—good men all, each worth a dozen common soldiers.

"Brothers, help comes riding swift as a prayer answered—but we must ensure there's still a town to defend when they arrive. I need volunteers to cross that bridge with me, to hold the enemy while others dismantle the crossing from the center. It's a journey without return, a path that leads only one direction."

I sensed his surprise and pride deep as a well as every man stepped forward without hesitation, including young Thomas, whose face showed no trace of fear, only determination etched in lines that should have held laughter instead of gravity.

"My sword is yours," Thomas declared, his chin lifted high despite the fatigue. "My life is yours if you have need of it."

Edmund's voice strengthened like forge-fire fed with fresh coal, carrying the weight of nobility in every carefully chosen word. "Then let them remember this day when bards sing tales by winter fires. Let them tell how courageous men stood against an army not for glory, not for conquest, but for those who cannot defend themselves from the darkness."

The men raised their weapons in salute, their spirits lifting with their blades. In their eyes, I saw the same fire that burned in Edmund's heart—unwavering commitment to protect the innocent, whatever cost might be demanded, whatever sacrifice might be required.

It was beautiful and terrible to behold.

* * *

Edmund's heart grew heavy as we entered the chapel where morning light filtered through stained glass, casting colored hues across the wounded who lay on makeshift beds. Some slept fitfully, others stared at the ceiling with eyes that had seen too much suffering.

Edmund knelt before the altar worn smooth by countless prayers, his calloused hands clasped around my hilt like a supplicant seeking blessing. His prayer carried no flowery words or grand declarations— just the simple, honest plea of a warrior preparing for his final battle.

"Lord, grant me the strength to protect those who cannot protect themselves. Watch over those I leave behind, and if this be my last dawn, let it be said I stood firm when standing was needed most."

As Edmund rose, Father James approached with Thomas at his side, the priest's weathered face creased with concern.

"Thomas, my boy," Father James gestured toward a door near the altar. "Could you fetch more bandages from the storage closet? We'll need them soon enough for the work that comes after the battle's ending."

I felt Edmund's pain spike sharply as winter wind as Thomas disappeared into the narrow closet, sunlight streaming through a thin window slit to illuminate the space barely large enough for a grown man.

In one fluid motion that spoke of terrible resolve, Edmund stepped forward and closed the heavy door shut, the lock clicking with finality that echoed like a death knell.

"Sir Edmund!" Thomas's muffled voice carried through the thick wood like a cry from the bottom of a deep well. "What are you doing? Let me out! Let me fight beside you!"

Edmund pressed his forehead against the door as if trying to touch a beloved face one last time. "I cannot, Thomas. You have your whole life ahead of you, a bright future. I won't watch you throw it away today for an old knight's final gesture."

"Please!" Thomas's fists pounded against the wood with desperate rhythm. "I can fight! I can help! Don't leave me behind!"

"You already have helped, more than you know." Edmund's voice cracked. "Forgive me, lad. Live well. Live a good and just life."

I felt Edmund's heart breaking like pottery dropped on stone as he turned away from Thomas's desperate pleas, each step toward the chapel door heavier than the last, weighted with love and loss in equal measure.

But sometimes love demands the hardest choices. Sometimes protecting those we care for means bearing their hatred if that's the price of their safety.

Edmund knew this truth in bones that ached with years and a heart that bore too many scars to count.

I watched as our small band crossed the bridge with determination burning in every heart like a sacred flame. A handful of soldiers began their grim work while others held the perimeter, mauls striking against the bridge's central supports with a rhythm steady as funeral drums. Each blow echoed across the water like thunder, a countdown to our final stand.

Edmund's grip tightened around my hilt as the war horns split the morning air, sharp as breaking glass. I felt no fear in Edmund—only fierce resolve as the enemy charged toward us in a dark wave of steel and fury that promised to wash away everything in its path.

We met them at the bridge's end, Edmund's bladework flowing like a master dancer's art. By his hand, I sang a deadly song with a voice clear and true, each strike purposeful as a prayer offered in a time of greatest need. His men fought with the strength of heroes, each one worth ten of the enemy. But even heroes fall when the numbers grow too great.

One by one, Edmund's brothers-in-arms fell around us like autumn leaves touched by a killing frost. His grief struck deeper than any blade at each loss, yet his own steel never faltered, never wavered from its purpose. The bridge groaned beneath us as the support beams splintered like kindling, the death throes of ancient stonework that had served in peace for countless years.

"For Valandria!" Edmund roared as the last support gave way with a sound like the world breaking. The bridge's center collapsed into the rushing river below. But we were now cut off, surrounded on the wrong side of the bank with nowhere to retreat except into death's patient arms.

Wounds appeared across Edmund's body like terrible flowers blooming—a slash here, a stab there, each one payment demanded for time bought with blood. Still, he fought on, each movement slower but no less determined.

I felt his life force ebbing like the tide retreating from the shore, yet his spirit burned brighter than ever—incandescent with nobility that no wound could touch, no death could diminish.

Through Edmund's fierce fighting, my attention was drawn to movement on the village side of the destroyed bridge. There, crouched behind an overturned barrel, a small boy watched our desperate battle with eyes wide as coins, terrified as a rabbit caught in an open field when hawks circle overhead.

His clothes were threadbare as hope worn thin, his face smudged with dirt and tears that spoke of too much fear for one so young. He couldn't have seen more than twelve summers, a child who should have fled with the other townspeople but somehow was overlooked in the chaos of evacuation.

The sight pierced my essence deeper than any physical blade could reach. Here was the very embodiment of what Edmund fought to protect—an innocent child who should never have to witness such violence, yet whose future hung upon this moment's bloody thread like a spider's web in a storm wind.

The boy's gaze locked with Edmund's for a heartbeat that stretched like eternity before I felt my wielder's resolve strengthen anew like bellows feeding forge-fire. Every moment we delayed the enemy from reaching that child was precious beyond gold, every second bought with blood meant another chance for safety to find its way to innocence.

A blade found its mark then, driving through Edmund's stomach with finality that rang like a funeral bell. Edmund fell to his knees, his grip on my hilt loosening like an autumn leaf releasing a tree, his fingers trembling against my steel.

Blood stained his tabard crimson as spilled wine, spreading like sunset across fabric that had known honor. Each labored rise of his chest sent ripples of agony through our shared consciousness like stones cast in a still pond.

Then we heard it—horns in the distance carrying the clear notes of Valandria's army, their brass voices piercing the gray dawn like shafts of golden sunlight breaking through storm clouds. Through our fading connection, I felt Edmund's lips curve into a smile, peaceful and serene despite the pain wracking his body like fire in his bones.

The town was saved. His sacrifice had bought the precious time needed for reinforcements to arrive, each minute paid for in drops of his noble blood freely given. Victory tasted sweet as honey despite the bitter dregs of approaching death.

As his life slipped away like water through cupped hands, the truth blazed through me like sacred fire that burns away all pretense, and I finally understood. This was love in its purest form—not the desperate clinging of a warrior seeking glory, not the cold calculation of a thief pursuing wealth's empty promise, but the willing sacrifice of one life for many.

In Edmund's final heartbeat, I felt the profound truth that would forever change my essence, burning away the last doubts like morning mist before the sun: there is no greater love than to lay down one's life for others who cannot defend themselves.

His death was not an ending but a testament to the highest calling a soul could answer. And in that moment, another piece of my purpose clicked into place like a key finding its lock—I existed not merely to reveal truth or protect the innocent, but to witness and carry forward the noblest acts of those who wielded me.

I was memory made steel, conscience forged in fire, a repository of wisdom earned through blood and sacrifice freely offered. In me lived the echo of every noble deed, every moment when someone chose light over darkness, others over self.

As Edmund's fingers slipped from my hilt for the final time, his blood pooled around us both like an offering poured out on an altar of sacrifice. The horns of Valandria's army grew louder like thunder rolling across the hills, but he would not live to see their banners flying in the victorious wind.

His eyes, clear and peaceful despite the pain that would have broken lesser souls, gazed skyward one final time toward the heaven that waited patiently as dawn. With his last breath that misted in the cool air, he whispered a prayer of gratitude—not for glory or recognition that feeds pride's hungry mouth, but for the simple blessing of having served well those who needed protection most.

The light faded from his eyes like a candle guttering out, but the brilliance of his sacrifice would illuminate my path forever, a beacon that could never be extinguished by darkness or doubt.

In dying, Edmund had taught me what it truly meant to be alive.

7

Of Corruption and Choices

I lay in Edmund's cold grasp until rough hands pried me from his noble fingers. Through a haze of grief, I felt myself lifted by a Malvorian captain whose touch fell foreign and harsh against my steel—cold where Edmund's had been warm.

His dark satisfaction rippled through our brief contact—triumph and greed mingling as he examined my craftsmanship. The Malvorian army retreated before the approaching Valandrian forces, carrying me as spoils of war away from the broken bridge.

"This blade belonged to their commander," the captain announced to his men as they rode. "King Burgund will be pleased with such a trophy."

The journey to Malvora's capital passed in a blur of motion and darkness. Days bled into nights as I changed hands, my grief making me numb. The memory of Edmund's final breath haunted me—that last whispered prayer, the light fading from eyes that had seen too much yet never lost their kindness.

Eventually, they threw me into a dank armory beneath the castle where moisture crept through stone walls and rust claimed lesser blades. The air tasted of neglect and forgotten purposes.

Time lost all meaning in that lightless place. I retreated deep within myself, replaying memories of Edmund's sacrifice, preserving his essence like a precious jewel. His courage, his love, his willingness to die for those who couldn't defend themselves—these became my treasures in that kingdom of shadows.

Seasons turned beyond my prison walls. Spiders wove webs between my crossguard, and rats scurried past. Other weapons came and went—swords drawn for battle and war, for ceremonies that celebrated conquest over justice—but I remained, gathering dust.

The only breaks in my solitude came when guards entered to retrieve weapons for training, their torches briefly illuminating my forgotten corner before darkness reclaimed me.

Then came different footsteps—lighter, more purposeful. Light flared as a servant held a torch high, illuminating shelves of forgotten arms.

He clutched a leather-bound book, its pages crackling like leaves trampled underfoot as he turned them. "This one here," he pointed toward me, speaking to workers who followed. "The king specifically requested it. Says it's to be a gift."

Rough hands lifted me from my resting place, and for the first time in years, I felt curiosity stir within my steel. Who would receive such a gift? What new wielder would shape the next chapter of my existence?

The servant's voice echoed off the stone walls. "Clean it thoroughly. Polish the steel until it shines. Replace the grip—see how the leather's rotted? His Majesty wants it to look as it did in its glory days."

Daylight blinded me as I was carried from the armory. The world had changed during my imprisonment—or perhaps Malvora simply differed so greatly from Valandria. Where Edmund's homeland had bustled with life and purpose, this kingdom seemed shrouded in quiet desperation.

The faces I glimpsed as I was carried through corridors showed the strain of hard years. Servants moved carefully, having learned that drawing attention brought trouble. Guards watched each other as much as they watched for threats.

I felt King Brackkus's trembling hands lift me from the velvet cushion. His touch radiated uncertainty and fear—emotions that clashed with the grandeur of his throne room.

Through our brief connection, I sensed the hollowness within him, a void where strength should dwell. His spirit felt brittle like a cracked eggshell, ready to crumble at the slightest pressure.

I searched his mind and witnessed how the defeat at Casterbridge had been the first break in Malvora's foundation. During my years of imprisonment, the kingdom had shattered beneath King Leofric's vengeance.

The price of their invasion had been paid in royal blood—King Burgund's life forfeit for his ambitions, his crown passing to a son who wore it without understanding its weight.

The years since had shown no healing. Malvora remained adrift, its people lost in the shadow of former glory, waiting for leadership that Brackkus seemed unable to provide.

The throne room reflected this decline. Tapestries hung faded and dusty, gold leaf flaked from once-proud columns, and the guards' armor showed patches of hasty repair. Even the courtiers' finery seemed worn at the edges as they watched their king with wary eyes.

The throne room doors creaked open, and shadows seemed to seep through the gap. A figure glided across the marble floor, black robes whispering against stone.

Sallow skin stretched tight across sharp cheekbones. His eyes, deep-set and black, seemed to devour light rather than reflect it. Lank, raven hair framed his gaunt face, falling past his shoulders like a funeral shroud.

Long fingers emerged from voluminous sleeves—spider-like and bloodless. The very air grew thick around him, heavy with an unseen presence that made my steel crawl.

Daygon. His name whispered through the throne room without being spoken.

The courtiers parted before him, their faces masks of deference that couldn't hide their terror. Even the guards stiffened, hands tightening on weapons they dared not draw.

"Ah, the legendary Truthseeker." His voice slithered through the air, each word carrying shadows that wrapped around the king's weak will. "You honor me with such a gift, Your Majesty."

"Will this truly—" Brackkus's voice cracked, and he cleared his throat. "Will this sword help us regain our glory? My kingdom crumbles each day."

Daygon's lips curved into something that might have been a smile. "My dear king, with this blade, your enemies will fall to their knees. Every kingdom that raises a sword against you will crumble like sand through your fingers."

Dark magic pulsed through each syllable, and I felt Brackkus's grip loosen. His hands shook as he extended me toward the sorcerer.

"Then take it, as we agreed." The words carried the weight of surrender.

Daygon's fingers closed around my hilt, and ice shot through my essence. His touch burned with ancient malice, centuries of cruel intentions crystallized into a single point of contact.

Visions flooded our connection—not possibilities but promises. Cities burning under starless skies. Children weeping as shadows consumed them. Thrones built from the bones of fallen kings.

I tried to withdraw, but his will clamped around mine. His consciousness probed at my essence, searching for weaknesses.

"Yes," he whispered, too softly for any but me to hear. "You will serve me well."

* * *

Daygon's footsteps echoed through the winding tower stairs. His chambers at the peak stretched across an entire floor, windows blocked by heavy curtains that writhed in unseen wind.

The walls crawled with shadows that shouldn't exist. Bottles of vile substances lined shelves between tomes bound in materials I dared not contemplate. Dried herbs hung from the ceiling—not healing plants but twisted things that grew where light feared to tread. At the room's center, a black altar bore deep scratches and stains that spoke of unspeakable rituals.

"At last." Daygon's voice dripped with satisfaction as he placed me upon the altar. "The final piece."

He moved between shelves, gathering components while muttering incantations that made my steel shudder. The air grew thick with magic that felt wrong, corrupting. Glass clinked against glass as he selected vials of liquid that glowed with sickly light.

"You see, Truthseeker," he spoke as he worked, "your power to reveal truth makes you perfect for my purposes. Once I bind you to my will, you'll help me chain Brackkus's soul to mine. That fool will become my puppet, dancing to my whims while believing himself in control."

I glimpsed his twisted vision—Malvora transformed into a kingdom of shadows, its people bent beneath his dark rule. Children weeping in streets where hope had died, warriors twisted into mindless thralls, and at its heart, Brackkus—a hollow shell through which Daygon's will would flow.

"And that's merely the beginning." His fingers traced Gregory's maker's mark, burning like acid against my creator's signature. "Once Malevora falls, other kingdoms will follow. The world will learn true darkness."

Never had I felt such evil—not even in the warrior's pride. This was malevolence distilled in its purest form, darkness that sought not just to corrupt but to destroy all that was good.

Daygon began inscribing runes along my blade with a brush dipped in black liquid that smoked where it touched my surface. Each symbol burned into my essence, attempting to overwrite the purpose Gregory had forged into me.

Each mark was a violation. The dark magic sought to remake me into something twisted, to transform an instrument of truth into a weapon of lies.

His cold fingers traced the final runes along my blade, dark magic seeping into my steel like poison. "Almost complete," he murmured. "Just one last ingredient needed."

He paused, lips curled into a cruel smile. When he spoke again, his words sent ripples of horror through my consciousness.

"The blood of an innocent child."

No. Throughout my existence, I'd witnessed death—warriors falling in battle, killers meeting violent ends. But this... this was different. This was the murder of innocence itself, evil undiluted by excuse.

Daygon's grip tightened as he swept me from his tower. His mount waited below—a black stallion whose eyes reflected its master's darkness.

* * *

For three days we journeyed eastward, Daygon's soldiers falling into formation behind us. Each day, Mount Valthoran grew larger on the horizon, its jagged peak a black tooth against the sky, the highest point in all Malvora. Local folk called it the Throne of Night, though they spoke such names in whispers.

At its base lay the village of Thornhaven—humble dwellings pressed against the mountain's roots, surrounded by towering pines.

I felt Daygon's anticipation building as we approached. The setting sun painted the peaceful scene in gold—children playing near the well, women hanging laundry, men returning from the fields.

None suspected the horror about to descend upon them.

"Take what you want," Daygon commanded his troops. "Kill any who resist. But bring me a child."

The soldiers surged forward like an evil tide. Screams shattered the evening calm as they kicked down doors and dragged people into the streets. Flames erupted from thatched roofs, smoke rising thick against the mountainside.

Daygon watched from horseback, eyes reflecting the burning village with terrible pleasure. Using me as a pointer, he directed his men toward homes that might harbor the prize he sought. Each time my tip aligned with a new target, shame burned through my steel.

Parents fought desperately to shield their children, only to be cut down. The village square ran red with innocent blood as Daygon's men executed their brutal search, hunting for the perfect sacrifice to complete his dark ritual.

I felt his satisfaction spike when he spotted a small boy—no older than five or six, with golden curls and an innocent face. The child had hidden behind a barrel.

Perfect for his vile purpose.

With serpentine speed, Daygon dismounted and snatched the screaming child.

"No! Please! Samuel!" the boy cried, tears streaming down his face.

We thundered up the mountain path. The boy's terrified sobs pierced my essence, each cry cutting deep within me.

At the summit, wind howled across the peak like death's hungry breath. Daygon bound the child's small wrists and ankles, laying him upon a flat rock that jutted over the burning village below.

Stars emerged in the darkening sky. He arranged black candles in a circle around the altar, their flames burning an unnatural purple. The child whimpered, trembling with fear and cold.

Approaching the cliff's edge, Daygon raised me high. Dark words slithered from his lips—ancient and forbidden syllables that made the air recoil. Magic crackled around us like black lightning as he turned, pointing my tip toward the weeping child.

And something inside me shattered.

All the pain, all the horror I'd witnessed crystallized into a single moment of pure defiance. Every memory of goodness—Gregory's loving hands, Sarah's gentle care, Elara's healing touch, Edmund's noble sacrifice—rose up like an army deep within me.

My essence exploded outward, negating his spell. For the first time since my forging, my voice broke through the barrier between steel and flesh.

"NEVER AGAIN!" My words thundered across the mountaintop, visible as ripples of blue light from my stell. "I am Truthseeker, forged in light and justice. No more shall my blade serve evil's purpose!"

Daygon's laughter cut through the air like shards of broken glass. "What can a mere sword do against its master? You are but a tool, and I am one of many who will wield you for darkness."

"I reject your mastery," my voice rang with certainty. "I am an instrument of truth and justice!"

Gregory's maker's mark began to pulse with azure light. The dark runes along my length started to smoke and hiss, burning away as my true nature reasserted itself.

My weight multiplied thousandfold, becoming heavy as the mountain itself. Daygon's grip failed, his fingers scraping uselessly against my suddenly burning-hot hilt as I plunged into the stone beneath us.

"No!" he shrieked. "You cannot defy me! You are just a thing!"

The cliff split with a thunderous crack, the sound echoing across the valleys like the judgment of heaven itself. Rock fractured beneath

Daygon's feet as he tumbled into the abyss, his scream fading into darkness.

The bound child lay at the edge of the breaking cliff. I could do nothing to save him as stone crumbled beneath us both—nothing but hope that someone would find him, that he would survive.

Our eyes met for the briefest moment before the ledge gave way completely.

As I fell alongside the cascading rocks, profound peace filled my essence. Better to be lost forever than serve evil's purpose again.

The impact came with a sound like thunder, driving me deep into the earth. Yet I summoned my power. The stone around my blade softened, then hardened again, sealing me within the rock.

From this day forward, I would choose my wielder. Only one worthy of the truth I carried would ever draw me forth again.

And so I waited, cradled in stone, for the one who would prove worthy of truth and light.

8

The Sword and the Shepherd

I awakened to sunlight warming my steel like a gentle hand on cold metal. The memories of that terrible night—the village aflame, the child's tears, Daygon's final scream—remained etched in my essence like scars on well-used leather. Here, halfway down the mountainside, I had found not imprisonment but sanctuary.

My blade stood plunged deep into ancient stone, three feet of steel buried so firmly that only my hilt and a hand's span remained visible. The rock had welcomed me, embraced me, as if this moment had been written in the mountain's bones since its birth.

Morning dew gathered on my crossguard. Birds nested in nearby trees, their songs filling the air with melodies that changed with the seasons. I watched seeds grow into saplings, wildflowers bloom and wither, the world spinning through its endless dance, while I remained steadfast in my chosen vigil.

The first to try claiming me was a merchant, silk robes rustling as he wrapped both hands around my hilt. Through his touch, I glimpsed his soul—ledgers thick with false numbers, workers cheated of honest wages, families driven to ruin by his greed. I remained unmoved as he strained and cursed, his face reddening until he finally released me with a disgusted snort.

"Rusted in place," he declared to his companions, though they could not see how I had weighed his heart and found it wanting.

A soldier discovered me next, his armor bearing Malvora's serpent crest. His hands burned against my hilt as I sensed the villages he'd razed, the innocents slaughtered for sport. I stayed firm as granite while he pulled until veins bulged in his neck.

"Some blacksmith's jest," he muttered, kicking the stone in frustration before stalking away empty-handed.

Children played near my resting place, weaving flower chains around my crossguard each spring. Their pure hearts held no desire to possess me, only wonder at my presence. Through their games and stories, I learned how tales of my defiance had grown in the telling.

Some claimed I was a gift from the Creator, thrust into the mountain to mark sacred ground. Others whispered I had fallen from the stars themselves. A few believed I was an ancient king's sword, waiting for his heir to return and reclaim what was rightfully his.

"The prophecy says only the true king can draw the sword," an old woman told wide-eyed children gathered at my base like flowers around a well. "One with a heart pure enough to rule with justice instead of greed."

The village below flourished into a proper town. My resting place became a landmark, a destination for travelers seeking to test their worth. Merchants, warriors, nobles—all tried their hand at drawing me forth. But I had learned to read the truth written in souls, to sense the darkness lurking behind grand gestures and honeyed words.

For thirteen years, I stood as a silent witness to humanity's nature— both its capacity for shadow and its potential for light. I waited, patient as stone, knowing that someday a worthy hand would grasp my hilt. Until then, the rock remained not my prison, but my choice, my sanctuary.

Through my stone embrace, I witnessed the daily theater unfold. Crowds gathered in ever-growing numbers, their excitement thick as morning porridge as each new challenger approached. Merchants had erected permanent stalls nearby, hawking everything from meat pies to trinkets carved with my likeness.

"Place your bets! Will today's contestant be the one?" The bookkeeper's voice rang out each morning, coins clinking as hopes and dreams changed hands like autumn leaves in the wind.

Knights in gleaming armor, mercenaries with scarred faces, nobles in fine silk—all came to test their mettle. Through each touch, I read their hearts like open books. One sought glory for glory's sake. Another dreamed of using my power to crush his rivals. A third simply wanted to sell me to the highest bidder.

The world beyond my resting place had descended into chaos. Whispers reached me of King Brackkus's fate—betrayed by his own family. Slain by his cousin, Lady Mira.

News of his death sparked wildfire across Malevora. Wealthy warlords raised private armies, each claiming divine right to rule. Villages burned like signal fires. Families fled their homes. The common folk suffered most, caught between warring nobles who cared nothing for their plight.

"Five years of bloodshed," an old woman muttered, warming her hands by a traveler's fire. "And for what? So some lord can sit on a fancy chair while children starve?"

I remained steadfast in my choice. Better to stay locked in stone than be wielded by hands stained with innocent blood. The realm needed more than strength or skill—it needed wisdom, compassion, and a heart untainted by the hunger for power.

Through the seasons, I remained firm, watching as men of all stations attempted to claim me. Each touch revealed their hearts, and each time I chose to remain unmoved, waiting for the one who would prove worthy.

* * *

Then one spring morning, a young man approached. Golden hair caught the sunlight like spun wheat, his slight frame and youthful face drawing jeers from the gathered crowd. Unlike the others who grabbed at me with greedy hands, he knelt before me with a gentle smile.

"It truly is you, Truthseeker."

His words sent lightning through my steel. This boy knew me.

He leaned closer, voice dropping to a whisper. "You are the sword that speaks. You are the sword forged in light and justice. You are the sword that saved me from evil as a boy." His eyes brightened with unshed tears. "Thank you."

Recognition flooded my memories like spring water breaking through winter ice—the child from that terrible night atop the mountain, now grown. *Merric* was his name. My being swelled with joy knowing he had survived, had thrived despite the darkness that had touched his young life.

As he touched my crossguard with reverent fingers, I felt the pure heart beating within him. His soul burned with the same righteous fire I'd known in Edmund—a passion for justice, a desire to protect the weak rather than exploit them. If I could have wept, I would have shed tears of gladness.

Merric rose and turned to leave, prompting mockery from the crowd.

"You waited in line all day just to not try pulling it?" a burly man called out, his laughter echoed by others who had nothing better to do than mock what they couldn't understand.

"The blade will budge when the blade decides to budge," Merric replied simply, continuing on his way as laughter followed him down the mountain path.

Something stirred within me—a righteous indignation I could no longer contain. My voice rang out across the mountainside, piercing the veil between steel and flesh: "Draw me!"

Silence fell like a dropped stone among the gathered crowds. Merric turned back, recognition lighting his face. "That's the voice I remember, the voice I could never forget."

He approached once more, this young man who had spent his morning tending sheep, now standing before destiny itself. His calloused hand wrapped around my hilt and with effortless grace— natural as sunrise breaking over distant hills—he lifted me free of the stone that had been my home for so many years.

The ancient rock released me willingly, like a parent letting go of a child whose time has come. Golden sunlight caught my blade as it emerged, and for a moment, the entire mountainside seemed to hold its breath. Then the crowd's shock erupted into wild cheers, their voices echoing off the cliffs like peals of joyous thunder.

They surged forward, lifting us both onto their shoulders in celebration, their weathered faces streaked with tears of joy and wonder.

* * *

Through our connection, memories flowed as Merric carried me along the winding forest path. Afternoon sun filtered through ancient oaks, casting dappled shadows across his face as he spoke of his past.

"I was just a baby when Samuel found me," Merric's voice carried warmth when speaking of his adoptive father. "Wrapped in nothing but a thin blanket, half-frozen in the snow. He always said it was divine providence that led him to that particular spot that night."

His fingers traced absent patterns along my crossguard as we walked. "Samuel had traveled far in his younger days, seen more of the world than most. But of all his tales, none captured my imagination like the story of Sir Edmund at Casterbridge."

My spirit stirred at the mention of Edmund's name, memories of that fateful battle rising within my steel like smoke from banked coals.

"Samuel would tell it on winter nights by the hearth—how Sir Edmund discovered the betrayal within the city's keep, how he rallied the townspeople when all seemed lost." Merric's voice took on the cadence of a well-loved tale. "He described how Edmund stood on that bridge, defending it against impossible odds so the innocent could escape. One man against an army, buying time with his own blood."

Each word sent ripples through my being, for I had been there, had felt Edmund's unwavering resolve even as his strength failed. I sensed Merric's deep admiration for that sacrifice.

"That story taught me what true nobility means," Merric continued. "Not titles or lands, but the willingness to stand between evil and the innocent, no matter the cost. Samuel said Edmund's example inspired him to take me in, to show the same kindness to others that Edmund showed that day."

Merric's heart quickened as we approached the modest cottage. Smoke curled from the chimney, and the scent of fresh-baked bread drifted through the evening air like a homecoming embrace.

"Sameul!" Merric called out. "I've brought someone special."

Samuel emerged from the doorway, peppered hair catching the last rays of sunlight. He wiped flour-covered hands on his apron, his weathered face creasing with concern at the sight of the blade in his son's grasp.

"A sword?" Samuel's brow furrowed. "Where did you—" His words died as recognition dawned across his features.

"This is Truthseeker," Merric held me forward. "The blade that saved me from Daygon that night on the mountain. Remember how I told you about the talking sword?"

The moment Samuel's weathered fingers touched my steel, memories cascaded through our connection. Not my memories, but his—vivid flashes of a life lived in Edmund's shadow.

I saw through Samuel's eyes that terrible day at Casterbridge. The acrid smoke, the clash of steel, the roar of an army descending upon the town. Samuel crouched behind barrels, frozen in terror as Edmund stood alone against the advancing horde. Blood streaked Edmund's armor, yet still he fought, buying precious seconds with each swing of his sword.

The images shifted like pages turning. Samuel grew older, stronger, donning a watchman's cloak in a bustling city. His rounds became a sacred duty—protecting the weak, just as Edmund had done. Pride swelled as he rose to sheriff, then constable, carrying Edmund's example in his heart like a treasured keepsake.

Dark memories followed—standing beside a fresh grave, his beloved wife taken by fever. The badge felt heavy then, meaningless without her smile to come home to. The open road called, and Samuel answered, tracking bounties across distant lands.

Until that snowy night, here in Malvora, changed everything. A baby's weak cry piercing the winter silence. Tiny fingers blue with cold, reaching from beneath a frost-covered blanket. In that moment, Samuel understood what Edmund had died protecting—the precious gift of life, the chance to make a difference.

The cottage, the garden, the peaceful years raising Merric—all of it flowed through his touch. Samuel had found his purpose not in grand battles, but in saving one small life, in passing on Edmund's legacy of courage and compassion.

"I remember you," Samuel whispered, voice thick with emotion. "On the bridge that day. You shone like sunlight on water, even through all the smoke and blood."

* * *

The first knock echoed through the cottage just as night was falling. Samuel opened the door to reveal a crowd gathering in the twilight, their faces a mix of hope and skepticism.

"Is it true?" A woman pushed forward, eyes bright with fervor. "The boy drew the sword from the stone?"

More voices joined the chorus, pressing against the doorway.

"The prophecy speaks of a true king arising!"

"Nonsense," a gruff voice cut through. "Look at him—he's barely more than a teenager. What does he know of ruling kingdoms?"

Merric's grip tightened on my hilt, uncertainty warring with determination in his heart. Samuel stepped between his son and the growing crowd like a shepherd protecting his flock.

"The boy's no king," a merchant sneered, adjusting his fine silk coat. "Just another peasant who got lucky."

"But the sword chose him!" A young girl pointed at me, eyes wide with wonder. "My father says that sword only accepts the worthy!"

"Worthy?" The merchant laughed, a sharp, yapping cackle. "To lead us against the warlords? To challenge Daygon's remaining pupils? This boy wouldn't last five minutes in real combat."

I felt Merric's heart steady, his initial fear giving way to something stronger—the quiet resolve that had first drawn me to him.

"I never claimed to be a king," Merric's clear voice silenced the crowd. "Or a savior. I'm just someone who wants to help, like others helped me when I needed it most."

The gathered villagers shifted uneasily, some nodding in approval, others turning away in disappointment. Their mixed reactions rippled through the evening air—hope and doubt, faith and fear, all swirling together in the growing darkness.

* * *

Merric's heart skipped as a thunderous voice boomed across the village square the next morning.

"Bring me the sword, boy, or watch these people die." The speaker strode into the morning light with a swagger that dared anyone to stop him, his men marching behind him, weapons drawn and faces hard as winter stone. Garrick the Grim, they called him, a behemoth whose reputation for cruelty stretched across three kingdoms. He stood nearly seven feet tall, his black armor making him seem more demon than man in the morning light.

Fear rippled through the crowd, but in Merric's heart, I sensed something else igniting—righteous fury that burned away all hesitation. My essence sang in response, memories of countless battles flowing through me to him. The shepherd boy seemed impossibly small before the mercenary's towering frame, yet his spine remained straight, his gaze unwavering.

Stand firm, I whispered into his mind. *You are not alone. I will help you.*

The mercenary charged with a roar that shook the earth, his greatsword cleaving air like a woodsman's axe. But where others might have faltered, Merric flowed like water around stone. I guided his movements, hundreds of years of combat knowledge merging with his natural grace. Steel met steel in a shower of sparks that lit the gathering dusk.

"Impossible," the mercenary snarled as Merric parried another crushing blow. "You're just a boy! A shepherd playing at swords! A lucky parry."

Through our bond, I shared within his mind the patterns I'd observed in countless duels—the slight shift of weight before a thrust, the tensing of shoulders before an overhead strike. Merric adapted instantly, turning his opponent's superior strength against him.

When the brute overextended on a wild swing, Merric struck. My blade found the gap in the mercenary's defense, drawing first blood.

The giant stumbled backward, clutching his arm. Shock registered on his face, then transformed into murderous rage.

With a bestial roar, Garrick charged forward, abandoning all technique for pure fury. His massive blade whistled through the air in deadly arcs, each blow carrying enough force to shatter stone. But Merric had taken the measure of his foe. As the giant's sword swept down in a killing stroke, the shepherd boy stepped inside his guard. My edge sang true, finding the weak point where leg armor joined hip. The giant's roar turned to a howl as he toppled, his massive frame crashing to earth like a fallen oak.

"This ends now," Merric declared, voice carrying across the square with quiet authority that belied his years. "Leave these people in peace."

The fallen giant's face twisted with rage and fear, his reputation shattered by a shepherd boy who refused to back down. He scrambled away, barking orders to his men as they retreated into the pale morning light, leaving their plunder behind.

Cheers erupted from the villagers. They gathered around us, voices rising in celebration. As they celebrated in the streets, I felt Merric's quiet pride—not in himself, but in knowing he had protected those who couldn't protect themselves.

In that moment, I understood why I had chosen him. Not for his skill with a blade, for he had no skill without me, but for his heart to protect people.

* * *

Whispers of unrest reached us from across the kingdom like sparrows carrying dark tidings. Tales of the sword and the shepherd boy spread through taverns and markets, each retelling more embellished than the last.

In his fortress of black stone, Warlord Kravik laughed when his spies brought news. "A shepherd boy with a famous blade? Let him play at being a hero. The throne will be won with armies, not children's stories."

From her mountain stronghold, Lady Mira dismissed the reports with a wave of her jeweled hand. "Fairy tales for the gullible. While they chase legends, we'll seize what's ours by right of blood and steel."

But Duke Aldrich, cunning and cautious in his coastal keep, saw differently. His soldiers came at dawn, their boots heavy on the dirt road leading to our village. Merric sensed them before they appeared—twenty men, steel glinting in the early light.

"By order of Duke Aldrich, rightful claimant to the throne," their captain announced to the gathering crowd, "the boy known as Merric is to surrender himself and the blade called Truthseeker."

Villagers pressed close around our home, faces tight with worry. Samuel stood in the doorway, his weathered hand on Merric's shoulder. Merric's resolve hardened like steel in quenching oil.

"The sword chose him fair and true!" someone shouted from the crowd.

The captain's face darkened. "The Duke's patience has limits. Hand over the boy and the blade, or we'll take them by force."

I felt Merric's heart—steady and sure despite his youth. Where others might have trembled before twenty hardened soldiers, his grip remained firm on my hilt. Not from pride or bloodlust, but from something purer—an unwavering commitment to shield those who needed protection.

"Stand down," the captain barked. "This is your final warning."

"I cannot," Merric's voice rang clear as a chapel bell. "These people are under my protection."

Steel sang as blades cleared scabbards. The villagers scattered, but Merric stood his ground. The first soldier charged. Merric moved like a dancer, my blade catching sunlight as we deflected the strike. Another attacked from behind, but we pivoted, letting their momentum carry them past. Each movement was measured, each parry precise—not to kill, but to disarm and disable.

"He fights like Sir Edmund himself," Samuel breathed, watching from the doorway.

Three soldiers lay groaning in the dirt, their weapons scattered. One of the fallen—a young soldier barely older than Merric himself—cried out in pain, clutching a dislocated shoulder. Without hesitation, Merric knelt beside him, sheathing me to free both hands.

"Easy, friend," Merric said gently, examining the injury. "This will hurt for just a moment." With practiced care—learned from Samuel, who'd mended many villagers' shoulders in his days—reset the shoulder with a quick, sure motion.

The young soldier stared up at him in wonder. "You... you helped me? But I just tried to capture you." "You're hurt," Merric replied simply, as if that explained everything.

The captain watched this exchange, his sword hand trembling. In all his years of soldiering, he had never seen an enemy tend to a fallen foe's wounds. The sight struck him like a physical blow—this was not the behavior of a pretender or rebel, but of someone who truly understood what it meant to lead.

The captain raised his hand, stopping his men's advance. "By the Light," he whispered. "The stories were true."

An old woman pushed through the crowd, voice trembling with emotion. "The Creator has sent us a defender at last. Just as the prophecies foretold—a pure heart wielding truth against darkness."

The remaining soldiers lowered their weapons, some dropping to their knees. Even the captain bowed his head. "Forgive us, young master. We were blind, but now we see."

Through our bond, I felt Merric's discomfort at their reverence. He had not sought worship or glory—only to protect those who needed protection. Yet as the soldiers pledged themselves to his cause, I sensed a deeper truth emerging.

Sometimes the greatest leaders are those who never sought to lead.

9

Of Thunder and Thrones

In the days following our clash with Duke Aldrich's men, I witnessed our village bloom like a garden after a long drought. Battle-weary soldiers arrived each dawn, their armor telling tales of service under different banners—some bearing scratches from skirmishes, others dented by heavier blows. I sensed Merric's quiet unease at the swelling numbers, like a shepherd watching his flock grow beyond what any fold could hold.

"I'm no leader," he confided to Samuel one evening, his fingers tracing my crossguard with the careful reverence of a boy learning his letters. Before us, the hearth's embers settled into sleep with soft whispers and gentle pops. "These men seek a king, but I'm trying to protect our home—nothing grander than that."

Samuel's weathered hand found Merric's shoulder, settling there like blessing and burden both. "Perhaps that's precisely why they follow. Kings who chase crowns rarely deserve to catch them."

The firelight danced in Merric's eyes as he gazed into the flames, wrestling with a destiny that had crept up quietly as a morning sunrise. Outside, the sounds of an impromptu camp grew nightly—more voices sharing bread and hope, more cookfires painting stories on the dark, more prayers whispered to stars that seemed to lean closer for the listening.

Among the arrivals came Captain Thorn, his face mapped with lines that spoke of conscience and consequence. When he knelt before Merric in the village square, the morning sun cast shadows long as memory across the packed earth, and villagers gathered like witnesses to some ancient rite.

"I've done terrible things," Thorn confessed, his head bowed low as a supplicant's. "Burned farms when families couldn't scrape together their taxes. Separated children from parents to fill the warlords' labor camps like cattle pens." His voice cracked like kindling. "Each night, their screams visit my dreams and haunt me. We need someone who understands that justice without mercy isn't justice at all—just vengeance wearing pretty clothes."

Through our bond, I felt Merric's heart answer Thorn's pain like bell to bell. The same compassion that had stayed his hand against Duke Aldrich's men now reached across the space between them, steady as candlelight in a drafty room.

"Stand up, Captain," Merric said, softly. "The past cannot be unwoven, but we can choose the pattern going forward."

That evening, Merric gathered soldiers and villagers alike beneath a tapestry of early stars. Torches flickered, illuminating faces that held hope and skepticism in equal measure. He stood upon a platform of simple planks—no throne, just honest wood that knew its purpose.

"We fight not for vengeance or the sweet taste of power," he declared, his young voice carrying the authority of absolute conviction. "But to protect those who cannot guard themselves. Our strength will be seasoned with mercy, our justice guided by compassion's steady hand."

The code he spoke was simple as morning porridge, yet profound as first light: Defend the helpless. Show mercy to the defeated. Seek justice, never vengeance. Protect life above all else. Serve others before self.

I felt the rightness of these words resonate through my steel like a tuning fork struck true. They echoed the principles Sir Edmund had lived by—and through Merric's touch, I sensed not the hunger of ambition, but the quiet acceptance of one who serves because service is needed.

* * *

I guided Merric's hands as he demonstrated the ancient dance of blade and balance to his gathered defenders. His movements flowed with grace that would have surprised those who remembered only the shepherd boy, each strike precise as a calligrapher's pen, each parry measured as a baker's recipe.

Balance lives at the heart of all things, I explained while thirty pairs of eyes tracked his every gesture like sunflowers following light. *Let my blade become more than steel—let it be thought made manifest, purpose given form.*

Through our connection flowed the accumulated wisdom of centuries of those who wielded me—Sir Edmund's devastating efficiency in battle, the subtle movements that had carried him through desperate hours when death wore many faces. These memories danced with teachings from countless masters who had held me through the turning years, each adding their harmony to this symphony of steel. Now, in Merric's patient hands, these ancient lessons found new voices in fresh hearts.

"There's something otherworldly about the lad," I heard one soldier murmur to his companion as they practiced the forms Merric had shown them. "No young man his age should carry such knowledge in his bones."

"Divine blessing," another agreed, wiping honest sweat from his brow. "The old prophecies speak of one chosen by heaven's grace."

Merric paused in his practice, turning to address the whispers with the gentle firmness of a master gardener explaining soil to seedlings. "I am no more touched by divinity than any of you. Whatever wisdom flows through me comes not from my own merit, but through God's grace freely given. I'm merely a vessel, hoping to be filled and used for His glory."

The humility in his voice rang true as temple bells through our bond. Where others might have claimed special blessing or divine appointment, Merric grasped a deeper truth—that strength flows not from the vessel, but from what fills it.

"The sword chose him for his heart," Captain Thorn declared, his scarred face solemn as carved stone. "Not for his bloodline or the breadth of his shoulders."

I felt Merric's quiet agreement. He sought not to build monuments to himself, but to prepare these souls to stand guard over what mattered most—just as Edmund had done, just as Samuel had taught him.

* * *

Before the scout finished his grim report, I sensed the shadow falling across Merric's spirit like clouds across harvest fields. The four warlords had joined their banners, each backed by Daygon's pupils— men who'd traded their humanity for the power to bend reality like heated iron. The numbers made my essence ring with cold warning: their combined hosts would wash over us like flood waters.

"They plan to strike through the northern pass," the scout reported, dust from hard riding still painting his weathered features. "Their forces gather like storm clouds, ready to strike."

Captain Thorn's face hardened like cooling metal. "We can't make our stand here. The village would be trampled to ash in such a battle."

"Agreed." Another captain slammed his fist on the war table, making the crude wooden markers jump. "But where? We're too few to face them on open ground where numbers give them the advantage."

The valley, I whispered into Merric's mind. *Before the pass narrows to its throat. Their numbers become a burden there, not a blessing.*

"Truthseeker suggests we meet them in the valley before the pass," Merric said, his finger tracing paths on their crude map like a storyteller following plot threads. "Here, where the land itself will help us channel their strength into weakness."

Uncertainty rippled through the gathered captains like wind through wheat. Their eyes danced between Merric and my steel, weighing legend against military wisdom like merchants testing coin.

"The sword speaks to you?" Captain Redmond's voice carried a note of skepticism. His weathered hand found his own ordinary blade—good steel, but steel that never awakened as I.

"Not in words that echo aloud in the ear," Merric replied, his fingers finding familiar comfort in my crossguard's embrace. "But in feelings and memories, in whispers from battles long settled to dust."

Captain Thorn nodded slowly as sunrise. "My brother spoke of Truthseeker—he fought at the battle of Casterbridge. He said it was an enchanted blade, and it gave Sir Edmund divine power."

"Superstition dressed in fine clothes," muttered another captain, though he kept his voice quiet enough to avoid direct challenge.

I felt Merric's quiet amusement at their bickering. He'd grown accustomed to such responses—the dance of doubt and wonder that followed wherever mystery walked hand-in-hand with the practical world.

"Whether the blade speaks matters less than what we've all witnessed," Captain Thorn said with the firmness of one who'd seen enough to know truth from tale. "There's more to Truthseeker than fine craftsmanship and sharp edges. How else could Merric show such skill at a young age?"

Agreement murmured through the gathered men like water finding its level. Even the skeptics couldn't deny what their own eyes had recorded—the strange rightness that had marked my choosing of Merric, the uncanny precision with which he wielded me.

"It's bold as brass," Thorn said at last, studying their rough map with the eye of a farmer reading weather signs. "But better than sitting here like rabbits in a known warren."

Dawn found us marching northward, our small army moving beneath Merric's banner—a mighty oak stretching toward a silver star, embroidered on a shield of deep blue by hands that understood the weight of symbols. The morning breeze caught the fabric, its message clear as church bells: strength rooted in righteousness, reaching ever skyward toward hope.

I watched sunrise paint the mountains in shades of amber and gold— the same peaks that had once known him as a child marked for sacrifice, now witnessing his passage as leader of men who chose to follow rather than flee.

The irony settled in my steel like good wine finding its proper vintage. How many banners had passed beneath these same mountains? Snarling beasts and bloodied swords, eagles and serpents and wolves— all claiming dominion through fear or force. Yet here we moved beneath the oak and star, seeking not to conquer but to preserve, not to take but to protect.

Through the narrow mountain pass our forces filed like a thread through a needle's eye. Granite cliffs towered above us, their faces scarred by ancient battles and carved by wind into shapes that might have been prayers written in stone. Our column stretched back like an iron river, flowing toward destiny with quiet purpose.

The valley opened before us—rolling plains stretching toward horizons that promised either triumph or tragedy, tall grass rippling like waves on a golden sea. Dark clouds gathered in the distance, their brooding mass heavy with the promise of storm and revelation. Lightning flickered within their depths, still too far to hear.

"No sign of the warlords' forces," Captain Redmond reported, scanning the empty expanse with eyes trained to read danger in the landscape. "We've arrived first to this dance."

Merric nodded, our minds already working like a master chess player seeing moves yet to be made. "Captain Thorn, begin our preparations. I want earthworks dug before that storm reaches us. Redmond, position archers where the ridgelines offer advantage."

He turned to grizzled Captain Blackwood, a man whose scars told stories of survival and sacrifice. "Gather your strongest men for special work. The pass behind us has weak points that the ancients never fully strengthened. If these warlords push us back, we'll bring the mountain down and bar their path forward."

The valley came alive with purpose. Shovels bit earth, wooden stakes rose from hastily dug trenches, supply wagons formed barriers against what was to come. We were preparing for victory while planning for necessity's harsh demands.

Merric approached Braxton, one of our most skilled weaponsmiths. "Would you sharpen Truthseeker? I want him ready for what's coming."

Through Braxton's skilled hands, I felt the whetstone's gentle caress, each stroke precise as a lover's touch. Beyond our defenses, dust clouds rose on the horizon like the breath of approaching giants. The darkening sky pressed down heavy as iron, while wind whipped through valley grass with increasing fury.

When the enemy host emerged from distance and dust, my essence sang with cold warning. Thousands upon thousands of boots trampled hope beneath them, their numbers seeming endless as winter nights. Four banners snapped in rising wind—the Crimson Hand, the Black Tower, the Serpent's Eye, and the Iron Crown.

Merric's grip remained steady as mountain stone as he lifted me from

Braxton's care and mounted his horse. Through our bond, I felt no fear in his heart—only the clear certainty of purpose refined in fire. We rode out with his captains to meet the warlords in the center of the soon-to-be battlefield.

* * *

The warlords towered over Merric as he dismounted before them, their armor gleaming with dark enchantments. Behind them loomed their warlocks, shadows writhing beneath hooded robes like smoke given malevolent purpose. The very air seemed to recoil from their presence, as if light itself had learned to fear their touch.

"So this is the boy who dares challenge us?" Warlord Kravik's laugh ground like millstones crushing grain. His massive frame cast shadows that seemed to devour hope. "Playing at war with his pretty magic sword?"

"Did you bring us all this way to surrender," sneered Lady Mira, her armor adorned with serpent scales that caught light and twisted it to cruel purposes, "or simply to die with style?"

"Neither." Merric's voice carried across the wind that had begun to taste of storm. "I came to offer you one chance to step back from this path."

The warlords' laughter boomed like thunder before the deluge. "Bold words from a boy," Kravik leaned forward in his saddle like a hawk studying prey. "Your head will grace my gates before the sun rises."

"Your armies will be scattered like chaff," hissed one of the warlocks, his voice carrying the chill of winter graves. "Your followers will feed the crows and teach the world the price of opposing us."

Merric waited with the patience of one who'd learned that wisdom often wears silence like armor. When their taunts finally spent themselves against the wind, he spoke with quiet finality.

"I offer you this one chance to surrender. This will be the only mercy spoken here today."

Their renewed laughter shook armor and rattled weapons, while their dark servants joined with hissing laughter. Merric inclined his head, accepting their answer without surprise or anger.

He swung into his saddle and we rode forward—not toward our own lines, but parallel to theirs, his eyes meeting those of common soldiers caught in their masters' web. I felt his heart surge with compassion for these men, pawns moved across a board they'd never been allowed to see.

"Look at me," Merric called out, his voice carrying on the wind that had begun to taste of lightning. "I am one boy with one sword, yet I stand before you unafraid. Do you know why?" He paused, letting the question settle like seed on fertile ground. "Because I fight for something greater than myself—greater than gold or power or the cruel whims of those who see you as tools to be used and discarded."

Lightning split the darkening sky as he continued. "Your masters feed on fear and grow fat on suffering. They care nothing for your families, your hopes, the dreams you whisper to your children at night. You are less than cattle to them—at least cattle get fed before slaughter."

Thunder rolled across the valley as Merric raised me high, my steel catching what little light pierced the gathering storm. "Today you face a choice: stand for justice or serve evil. My men and I know what we defend. We know that if we fall here, we fall as free men."

He wheeled his horse, his final words cutting through the wind that now howled with purpose. "Can you say the same?"

Without waiting for a response, he rode back toward our lines, leaving heavy silence in his wake as the first drops of rain began to fall like tears for what was to come.

I felt Merric's heart beating steady as he faced his assembled troops. Rain misted down gentle as a blessing, catching in his hair like a crown of diamonds. His voice carried clear across the lines, cutting through the wind that had now found its voice.

"Look to your left, to your right! These are not merely fellow soldiers—they are brothers, fathers, sons. We stand here not as an army, but as a family bound by choice and conviction!"

Lightning split the sky, illuminating faces that bore the light of those who'd found something worth dying for.

"Think of the children in our villages who will speak of this day in years to come! Will they tell tales of how we cowered before evil's advance? Or will they sing of how ordinary folk became heroes? How farmers and craftsmen stood shoulder to shoulder with trained soldiers and declared 'No more!' to tyranny's reign?"

Thunder answered his words like heaven's own agreement.

"This storm that gathers—it carries no curse but heaven's blessing! Too long have these lands bent beneath shadow's weight. Today, we wash them clean! Today, we fight not for glory or gold, but for every mother who's lost a child to these tyrants! For every father who's watched his life's work burn! For every little one who's learned to fear the dark!"

A cheer rose from the ranks, building like the approaching storm, voices joining voices until the very air vibrated with purpose.

"Together we are lightning that strikes! Together we are thunder that shakes foundations! Together we will forge a realm worthy of our children's children!"

The answering roar drowned even the thunder's voice. Weapons beat against shields in rhythm that matched the storm's own heartbeat.

Enemy horns bellowed across the field like great beasts announcing hunger. Rain fell harder now, drumming against armor and turning earth to mud that would drink deep before day's end.

"The storm has arrived," Thorn observed from his mount beside us, his weathered face calm as an unmovable stone.

"Good," Merric's voice held a quiet smile. "Let it wash away what was and water the seeds of what's to come."

* * *

Steel sang against steel as enemy lines crashed against our defenses like a tide against a stubborn shore. Rain pelted down in sheets, turning the world to gray haze where motion and violence danced their ancient duet. The air was filled with screams and battle cries.

Our men held firm at first, but numbers began to tell their tale as they always do. For every enemy warrior who fell, three more stepped forward to fill the gap. Blood mixed with mud beneath countless feet as battle lines swayed like wheat before storm winds.

"Hold fast!" Merric's voice carried above the chaos like beacon fire in a fog. "Stand together!"

A warlock's spell burst against our shields, sending good men sprawling. Through Merric's grip, I felt his determination as we deflected another assault of corrupted magic, my steel singing with the impact of forces that sought to annihilate.

Then came thunder that shook the earth—hundreds of mounted warriors emerging from the storm's embrace on our right flank. Their charge would have rolled up our lines like parchment before flame, but nature herself intervened with irony sharp as any blade.

Rain had transformed the hillside to treacherous mud that caught hooves and turned certain death into confused stumbling. Warhorses slipped and fell, creating chaos where there should have been slaughter. Our archers seized the moment, sending volleys that turned retreat into rout.

Captain Thorn charged past us, his blade carving through enemy ranks like a farmer's scythe through wheat. The veteran warrior moved with deadly grace, each strike precise and devastating. Three warriors fell before they could even raise their shields.

Captain Redmond proved why men called him "Storm Dancer," his twin blades catching a warlock's lightning and sending it back like a gift returned unopened. The backlash scattered dark-armored soldiers like leaves before a gale.

But then malevolent energy crackled through rain-heavy air, and from the chaos emerged a hooded figure whose very presence made my steel vibrate with warning.

"Face me, boy," the warlock's voice rasped like dead leaves underfoot. "Let's test whether your famous blade can stand against power that bends reality to its will."

Merric stepped forward, his grip on my hilt unwavering as mountain stone. We moved as one when corrupted lightning sought us, my blade catching the energy and dispersing it harmlessly into hungry mud.

The warlock summoned writhing tentacles of shadow that had never known light's touch, but Merric had faced darkness before. We danced through his magical assault, closing distance with each step despite his increasingly desperate spells.

When steel met corrupted steel in a shower of sparks, I felt the difference between power drawn from hatred and strength that flowed from protection's well. With a cry that rose above the storm's voice, Merric struck true, and I cut through both blade and sorcery to find the dead heart that had forgotten how to beat with love.

As the warlock fell, his body dissolving like smoke before the wind, movement rippled through enemy ranks—a captain breaking away, his mud-splattered armor bearing the insignia of the Iron Crown.

"We choose to die as free men!" His voice carried across battlefield chaos. "My troops follow the one who wields truth!"

Thousands more followed his example, breaking ranks to join our cause. Their former masters' curses rode the wind, but the converts took position beside our warriors with faces that spoke of souls catching their second breath.

Merric raised me high, my blade catching what light pierced the storm. "Forward! Take the battle to them!"

As armies reformed their lines, the very heavens seemed to answer righteousness with favor. Lightning erupted from storm clouds, striking enemy ranks with precision that spoke of divine artillery. Each bolt illuminated the field in stark relief, sending enemy soldiers scattering like guilt before truth.

Through curtains of rain, the warlords themselves advanced with what remained of forces once thought invincible.

Merric stepped forward, raising me once more. His voice cut through the storm like a blade through silk: "For hope! For justice! For light that drives back the darkness!"

Our combined armies began their advance, boots striking mud in perfect rhythm, moving toward destiny head-on.

Lightning illuminated carnage in stark flashes as our forces crashed together like opposing tides. Through Merric's hands, I sang my ancient song of defense and justice.

Through tempest's fury emerged Warlord Kravik—a titan in black plate whose very presence seemed to devour hope. His greatsword hummed with dark enchantments.

"Face me, boy!" Kravik's voice boomed like collapsing mountains. "Let's end this farce!"

Steel met steel with force enough to shatter lesser blades. I caught his blow and redirected its power into the earth that drank violence like parched ground drinks rain. Where Kravik relied on brute strength, Merric slid forward like water carving its way between rocks.

"Stand still and die!" Kravik roared in frustration as another mighty swing found only empty air. Our duel intensified beneath lightning's strobing witness. Dark magic trailed from Kravik's blade like smoke from funeral pyres, but my steel sang purer notes that cut through corruption's symphony.

When our blades locked, I felt the void where his honor should have dwelt—emptiness filled only with hunger for power over others. But before Kravik could press his advantage, shadow materialized beside us.

His warlock struck with sickly green flames that found their mark despite our guard. Pain lanced through our connection as Merric fell to one knee, blood mixing with rain on his battered armor. Kravik raised his sword for the killing blow, dark satisfaction twisting his features.

But in that moment of extremity, something extraordinary flowed through our bond—every noble memory I'd gathered across my years surged into Merric's spirit like a dam-burst river. Sir Edmund's sacrifice, Elara's compassion, the pure hearts of all who'd wielded me for justice rather than gain.

We moved faster than thought itself. My blade swept up to catch the warlock's spell and reflected it back. Green fire consumed its caster as I cut through Kravik's corrupted blade to find the black heart that had forgotten how to love anything but power.

The warlord's eyes widened in disbelief as he toppled backward into the mud. His final breath escaped in a rattle of confusion.

"The Black Tower has fallen!" The cry spread through our lines like wildfire. "Forward! Forward with Merric!"

Our men crashed into the enemy with renewed fury. Those who had hesitated now fought with the certainty of divine purpose. Farmers wielding pitchforks moved with the precision of trained soldiers. Merchants who had never held a blade struck with deadly accuracy. I witnessed ordinary men transformed by extraordinary courage.

Captain Thorn led a charge that shattered the enemy's left flank. His voice carried above the storm: "For truth! For justice!" Each swing of his blade inspired those around him to greater feats of valor.

Even the soldiers who had defected to our side earlier fought with increased determination. Their former comrades fell back before their onslaught, unable to stand against the conviction in their eyes. Where doubt had lingered in their hearts, now burned the fire of righteous purpose.

Through rain and chaos, I sensed them gathering—three warlords and their remaining dark servants, their combined malice like a void in the storm's heart.

This must end now, I whispered to Merric. *We must face them together, or watch good souls fall until none remain to remember why we fought.*

"What are our chances?" he asked, gripping my hilt with hands that trembled from exhaustion but not fear.

Slim. The dark magic they wield... it could destroy us both.

Merric's resolve flowed pure and unwavering through our connection. "If my death buys their lives, it's well spent."

We moved through the battlefield, my essence guiding Merric's steps. Their presence grew stronger—a malevolent pulse that made my steel shiver. Through the rain and chaos, I sensed them: three remaining warlords surrounded by their dark spellcasters, their combined power a beacon of evil in the storm-wracked field.

Merric's heart steadied as we approached the remaining warlords. Lord Vane of the Crimson Hand stood tallest among them, his armor stained the color of dried blood, a crown of roses adorning his helm. Beside him, Lady Mira of the Serpent's Eye coiled like a viper ready to strike, scales of enchanted metal gleaming beneath her dark cloak. Duke Aldrich of the Iron Crown completed their trinity of evil, his ornate armor bearing the weight of a hundred cruel victories.

"The boy who would be king," Lady Mira's voice dripped with venom. "Look how he bleeds already."

"Kravik was always the weakest among us," Lord Vane spat, drawing his crimson blade. "We won't be easy prey."

I sensed their hatred—not just for Merric, but for everything he represented. Hope. Justice. The light that threatened to expose their corruption.

Before them, Merric knelt and planted my point in mud that would witness either our triumph or our ending. Rain trickled down my blade as his prayer began, soft yet carrying the weight of absolute faith.

"Creator in Heaven, I lift up those who've fallen defending what matters most. Let their sacrifice water seeds of justice. And for those who still fight—grant them strength not for glory's sake, but to serve Your purposes in a world that needs light more than darkness."

His words stirred something deep in my essence. Through centuries of questions about purpose and meaning, understanding finally bloomed like a flower after a long winter. I knew I wasn't forged merely to take life or win battles, but to reveal truth. I was meant to help those who wielded me see past their own doubts to the light within. To be a mirror reflecting the Creator's truth, for He is truth itself.

Merric rose, his grip firm on my hilt as he assumed a fighting stance. I felt his spirit aligned perfectly with this revelation—a vessel of truth facing down evil.

Lady Mira struck first, her enchanted blade whistling through the rain. We parried, my steel singing against her corrupted metal. Lord Vane's crimson sword joined the dance, forcing us to weave between their coordinated strikes.

The warlocks unleashed their power—bolts of shadow and sickly green flame cutting through the storm. Yet where their magic sought to corrupt, my essence rejected it. Each clash of steel sent sparks cascading like fallen stars, illuminating the faces of soldiers who had ceased their fighting to witness this confrontation.

Duke Aldrich's mighty war hammer crashed down, cratering the earth where we had stood moments before. Merric rolled, bringing me up to deflect Lady Mira's follow-up strike. I guided his movements yet this seemed barely enough against such overwhelming odds.

Lightning split the sky as all three warlords pressed their attack simultaneously. Their blades became a whirlwind of death, while the warlocks wove increasingly powerful spells. The very air crackled with conflicting energies—their darkness against my light, their corruption against our truth.

A warlock's spell caught Merric's leg, sending him stumbling. Lord Vane's blade opened a gash across his shoulder. Blood mixed with rain as he struggled to maintain his guard. Lady Mira's enchanted sword slipped past our defense, drawing another line of red across his ribs.

The gathered soldiers—friend and foe alike—watched in stunned silence as Merric fought on. Despite his wounds, despite the overwhelming odds, he refused to yield. Yet I felt his strength ebbing through our bond, his movements growing slower with each exchange.

Duke Aldrich's hammer struck again, this time catching Merric's side with a sickening crack. He fell to one knee, using my point for balance as the Warlords closed in for the kill. Their dark laughter mingled with the thunder as they raised their weapons for the final strike.

Then the music began—divine harmonies filling my essence despite battle's chaos. Time seemed to slow, the raindrops hanging suspended in the air like diamonds.

The melody was not music, but voices—hundreds of them, layered in perfect harmony. I recognized them as prayers, rising like incense from distant homes and hearths. A mother's desperate plea for her son's safety. Children begging for their father's return. Wives and sisters calling out to heaven for protection.

Even here on the battlefield, silent prayers joined the chorus. Wounded soldiers clutching keepsakes, warriors gripping weapons with white-knuckled hands—all adding their voices to the symphony of supplication.

Then, cutting through the celestial chorus, came another voice—softer than a whisper, yet more powerful than thunder. It spoke directly to my spirit, revealing truths I had glimpsed but never fully grasped. About my purpose, about divine power flowing through willing vessels, about truth being stronger than any darkness.

"I understand," I whispered into the sacred stillness.

Stand! I called to Merric. *Raise me to the sky!*

Though pain wracked his frame, his spirit answered. With trembling arms that found sudden strength, he lifted me skyward as golden lightning split storm clouds to strike my steel with divine force.

Power coursed through me into Merric, healing wounds and filling him with celestial fire. My essence transformed, crackling with holy lightning that made the very air sing truth's ancient song.

We advanced through spells that dissipated like smoke before dawn. Lady Mira's enchanted blade shattered against my lightning-wreathed edge before divine fire consumed her. Lord Vane fell to the lightning that erupted from my point. The warlocks crumbled to ash before heaven's wrath.

Duke Aldrich's desperate hammer blow met only empty air as my edge found his corrupted heart, holy power purging evil that had festered too long in mortal flesh.

As the last enemy fell, sunlight pierced storm clouds like a sword through silk. Throughout the field, remaining enemy soldiers dropped weapons or fled in terror. Victory's song rose from our ranks—not triumph over conquest, but celebration of light preserved against shadow's advance.

* * *

Months later, we approached the capital's towering walls, most strongholds having surrendered at the sight of Merric's standard.

"Who comes to our gates?" a knight called down from the battlements, his armor reflecting the morning sun.

109

Captain Thorn's voice rang clear across the morning air. "This is Merric Lightbringer, who struck down the warlords with heaven's light!"

The massive gates groaned open, revealing an elderly man in fine robes. "Welcome, my lord. I am Steward Aldwin. Please, follow me."

As we rode through the streets, the city erupted in celebration. People hung blue banners from every window, waved blue cloths, and even threw blue flower petals before our horses. Their voices joined in song that echoed off the stone walls:

"The warlords came with darkness fell, Ten thousand strong they stood! But King Merric struck with heaven's light, And evil's reign he would end! Ten thousand fell before his sword, When truth blazed in his hand!"

The crowd grew as we approached the castle, following like a jubilant tide. In the grand courtyard, Steward Aldwin lifted a simple golden crown.

"The people have chosen," he declared, placing it upon Merric's head.

Merric stepped forward, his heart steady. "I never sought a crown," his voice carried across the courtyard. "But I accept this burden as a sacred trust. I vow to serve you with compassion, to rule with mercy, to be a shepherd rather than a tyrant."

Raising me high in sunlight that caught my steel like captured starfire, he declared: "Let this mark a new beginning! No longer shall this land bear the name Malvora—place of evil. From this day forward, we are Luminara—the realm of light!"

The people's cheers shook the very stones of the castle. As they celebrated, I felt Merric's quiet resolve through our bond. Not pride in victory, but determination to fulfill the sacred trust placed in his hands.

In that moment, I understood my own journey more clearly. Through countless hands and hearts, I had sought my purpose. Now I realized that purpose was not fixed but evolving—to reveal truth, to defend justice, to guide those who wielded me toward their highest calling.

Like Merric, I had never sought greatness. But in serving truth faithfully, we had both found something greater than glory—we had found purpose. And in that purpose, we had found peace.

10

The Journey Home

Thirty years passed like pages turning in a well-loved book—
each one precious, none forgotten. I watched Merric's
children grow from babes who gurgled at my gleaming surface
to strong young folk who carried their father's gentle spirit like
heirloom cloaks passed down through generations. His marriage to
Edith, Captain Thorn's youngest daughter, brought joy that radiated
through our bond like warmth from a well-tended hearth.

The kingdom flourished under his shepherd's care, transforming
from shadow-haunted wasteland into something that made travelers
pause and smile without quite knowing why. Folk had taken to calling
him the Shepherd King—not from flattery, but from the simple truth
that he tended his people like a faithful shepherd tends his flock. Where
other rulers built monuments tall as their pride, Merric built shelters
for those who had none. Where they feasted in halls grand as cathedrals,
he shared his table with farmers whose hands bore earth's honest stains
and craftsmen whose fingers knew the language of creation.

The name suited him like a coat cut by loving hands. Just as a shepherd
leaves ninety-nine sheep to find one lost lamb, Merric would travel any
distance—over hill and through valley, past comfortable castles and

through muddy villages—to aid even the humblest settlement that sent word of need.

But lately, my essence had begun to fade like candlelight when a window opens. Each day brought diminishment, a gentle ebbing that whispered of journeys ending and circles closing. The divine fire that had once coursed through my steel like bottled lightning grew dimmer, calling me back to where sparks first danced and metal sang.

One quiet evening, as Merric polished my blade in his study with the patient care of one tending an old friend, I spoke the words that had been gathering in my heart like dew.

My friend, my time grows short. I desire to return home—to the place where Sir Gregory first breathed life into my cold steel.

Merric's hands stilled on my surface like a prayer pausing between verses. Firelight caught the silver threading in his dark hair. "You wish to return to your birthplace?"

Yes. Something calls me there—deeper than memory, stronger than longing.

"Then we shall take that path together." His voice held the certainty of one who'd learned that love sometimes asks hard things of those who practice it faithfully. "You've served without counting the cost for three decades. Let me help you find your way home."

The next morning found Merric gathering a small company like a shepherd choosing his most trusted dogs—loyal knights whose hearts he knew, and two of his eldest sons whose steady spirits could weather whatever storms lay ahead. Through our bond, I felt his determination as he announced their mission to the assembled party.

"Truthseeker guided me when I was but a boy with more courage than sense," he declared, royal robes catching morning light that streamed through windows. "Now comes my turn to guide him home."

Thank you, I whispered into his mind. *For understanding what words can barely hold.*

"How could I not?" His fingers traced my crossguard with the tenderness of one touching a beloved face. "You've been more than sword or weapon—you've been my truest companion through shadow and light."

* * *

I gazed upon Casterbridge, my heart stirring like old coals touched by a gentle wind. The town had barely changed since that day nearly sixty years past when Edmund fell defending strangers who became family in his final hour. The same stone buildings lined streets worn smooth by countless honest footsteps, their weathered faces speaking of endurance that outlasts the storms.

Only the bridge stood different—rebuilt stronger and grander than before, like hope restored after sorrow's long winter.

As we approached, my essence surged at the sight of Edmund's statue standing guard at the bridge's entrance. Carved in marble white as morning clouds, he stood as memory had preserved him—proud yet humble, strength seasoned with compassion's salt. The inscription beneath caught the sunlight: "Sir Edmund, Hero of Casterbridge—Who gave his life defending the innocent. Forever honored by the Kingdom of Valandria."

Memories flooded through me swift as mountain streams after rain—Edmund's unwavering courage as he held the bridge like an oak holding ground against a gale, his final thoughts dwelling not on glory's bright baubles but on the townspeople whose faces had become dear to him. I remembered the weight of his last breath, the peace that settled over his heart as he fell.

Merric's hand tightened on my hilt as my remembrance flowed through our bond. "He was a great man," he whispered. "You must miss him deeply."

I do, I replied. *Missing someone... it was once such a foreign concept to me. A sword isn't meant to form attachments, to yearn for voices now silent. But through the centuries, I've learned that understanding loss is part of understanding love.*

Merric's own heart stirred with compassion, his spirit embracing my bittersweet remembrance like arms around a grieving friend. Together we stood in silence before Edmund's memorial, honoring a hero whose sacrifice had shaped paths we could never have walked alone.

Young Roland's concern rippled outward like stones cast in still water. His hand found his sword hilt—not in threat, but in the nervous habit of one learning to carry responsibility's weight.

"Father," Roland's voice bore traces of the diplomatic training that would one day serve his own kingdom. "Entering Valandria unannounced... surely the protocols demand—"

Merric's quiet chuckle warmed the space between them. "My son, look at us with clear eyes." He gestured to their simple traveling clothes—worn leather and rough-spun wool that had replaced royal finery. "Do you see a king and his princes? Or merely wanderers on the road?"

"But if we're discovered—"

"Then we'll meet that bridge when we come to it." Merric's fingers traced familiar patterns along my crossguard. "Sometimes the simplest path proves truest. No fanfare, no ceremony—just honest folk walking honest roads."

"Where does our path lead next, old friend?" Merric questioned.

To Valandria's heart, I replied, feeling the pull like a needle seeking true north. *To the center of Edmund's beloved kingdom.*

Merric's laughter echoed off stone buildings. "Perhaps I spoke too quickly about simplicity." I felt his mind already working—calculating how to navigate the realm's most guarded city while keeping their true nature hidden like precious things wrapped in common cloth.

* * *

After we had arrived at Veladorn, the bustling capital, our party sought rest and food at a nearby tavern. It embraced us with warmth born of human fellowship and good fire crackling on the hearth. Dozens of bodies created comfort against evening's spring chill, while our party sought rest at a table far from curious eyes and wagging tongues.

A serving maid bright as candlelight brought foaming tankards of ale, her smile lively and infectious. Musicians in the corner coaxed lively tunes from fiddles and drums, setting feet tapping throughout the room like raindrops finding rhythm. Laughter and conversation flowed freely as the evening's ale, creating the particular contentment that comes when honest folk gather after honest work.

The front door creaked open, admitting a soldier whose bearing spoke of decades spent in service to something greater than himself. His hair was white as moonlight on water, his frame remained strong—muscles carved by years of training rather than softened by comfort's easy chair.

Something about him tugged at my essence like a half-remembered melody. He settled at a nearby table with his companions, sharing tales and drinks with the easy camaraderie of men who'd stood together when standing mattered most.

His eyes, one of which had a small scar above it, drifted occasionally to our quiet corner, lingering with an expression.

When he passed our table later in the evening, his gaze fell upon me, where I rested against Merric's chair. He froze mid-step, color draining from his face as though he'd seen spirits walking among the living. His hands trembled as he stared at my blade.

"Is everything well, friend?" Merric's voice carried the genuine concern of one shepherd recognizing another's distress.

The soldier started like one waking from a deep dream, shaking himself from wherever memory had carried him. "Forgive me," he mumbled, hurrying past our table like one fleeing ghosts.

After the warmth of food and fellowship had settled into contentment, Merric found his rest on the straw-filled mattress in our rented chamber. Roland and Edgar had barely removed their boots when gentle rapping at the door sent them reaching for weapons with the instinctive care of those trained to protect what matters most.

Merric approached the door with caution wrapped in courtesy, opening it just enough to reveal the soldier from earlier. Candlelight from the hallway painted deep shadows across features.

"Forgive the late hour," the soldier whispered, bowing with respect. "But I must speak with you."

Something in the old man's earnest manner moved Merric to step aside and grant entry, like recognizing a kindred spirit beneath unfamiliar clothes.

The soldier's eyes found me immediately, where I rested against the wall. "May I... might I see your sword, sir?"

"Why do you ask?" Merric's tone remained gentle, but carried the wariness of one who'd learned to listen before trusting.

"Years past, when I was but a boy learning the weight of duty, my master carried a blade exactly like this one." The soldier's voice trembled like a bow across a heartstring. "The same distinctive crossguard, the same gleam that catches light and holds it like captured starfire..."

"Who was your master?"

A smile of pure devotion transformed his weathered features like a sunrise breaking over mountains. "Sir Edmund, the Hero of Casterbridge."

My essence surged with recognition, swift as lightning finding earth. Memories flooded through me—a young squire practicing forms in morning light, Edmund's patient instruction, the boy's unwavering loyalty during those final hours when courage was all any of them possessed.

Thomas. This was Thomas, the squire Edmund had locked in the church closet on the day death came calling, protecting him like a shepherd protecting a lamb from wolves.

The rush of remembrance flowed through my connection with Merric, showing him the brave heart this aged warrior had carried through all his years. Through our bond, I felt Merric's wonder as he witnessed Thomas's dedication to Edmund, saw the pure spirit that still beat beneath the soldier's graying hair.

"Your name is Thomas," Merric said with the certainty of one reading familiar text.

The old soldier stiffened like one caught in unexpected truth. "Yes... but how could you possibly know?"

"This is Truthseeker, the same blade that served with your master Sir Edmund. He revealed your name to me."

"Who revealed my name?" Thomas's brow furrowed like one trying to solve riddles.

"Truthseeker did."

Wonder and confusion warred in Thomas's weathered features as Merric crossed the room and lifted me from my resting place. He extended me toward Thomas with reverence usually reserved for sacred things.

The moment Thomas's callused fingers—scarred by years of honest duty—touched my steel, I opened memory's floodgates between us. I showed him that day in the armory, his young face bright with excitement as he pointed me out to Edmund like a child showing treasure to a beloved father. The many dawn training sessions where Edmund taught him balance and form with patience that never counted cost. Then that final, heart-rending moment when Edmund locked him in the church closet, protecting him from battle's harvest with love stronger than duty's call.

"Thank you," Thomas whispered, tears gathering in eyes that had seen too much yet somehow remained kind. "For showing me these precious moments. Edmund always said you were more than blade or steel. Now I finally understand."

Edmund loved you like a younger brother, I spoke into his mind. *You brought light to his days when shadows gathered thick.*

Tears spilled down Thomas's cheeks like rain after a long drought as he carefully handed me back to Merric's waiting arms. "Thank you for allowing me this moment. What brings you to the capital?"

"Truthseeker seeks his way back to where his story began," Merric explained. "I guide his final journey."

Before releasing his grip on my hilt, I shared one last truth with Thomas. *This man who wields me now is King Merric Lightbringer of Luminara.*

Thomas dropped to his knees like grain before a sickle. "Your Majesty! Forgive my informal manner!"

Merric's laughter filled the room. "Please, rise. I travel not as king draped in ceremony, but as a simple wanderer on the road."

"May I... might I join your quest to bring Truthseeker home?"

Yes, I whispered into both their minds. *You should journey with us.*

* * *

Dawn painted cobblestones in pale gold like coins scattered by generous hands as we prepared for departure. Stable boys brought forth horses whose breath steamed in the morning air, while Roland and Edgar secured provisions with the careful thoroughness.

Thomas appeared in armor polished to mirror brightness, catching the morning light.

"Before we take to the road," he said softly, "there's something I would like to show Truthseeker."

Through Merric's borrowed consent, Thomas led our small party

119

through Veladorn's waking streets—past markets coming to life like flowers opening to sun, past chapels opening doors to morning prayer. We approached the castle grounds, but rather than turning toward the main gate, Thomas guided us along a tree-lined path that opened like a secret door into magnificence.

Roses climbed marble columns like prayers ascending, while fountains sang gentle songs to the morning air. At the garden's heart stood a pavilion of white stone, its graceful arches reaching skyward. As we drew closer, I saw what lay within—a tomb of polished marble, carved with such skill it seemed to capture light itself and hold it like a precious gift.

Thomas raised his hand with reverence. "Here Sir Edmund rests."

Emotion swept through me like rain cascading off a roof—so powerful that Merric gasped, tears springing unbidden to his eyes. Joy and sorrow mingled like honey and salt, grief for what was lost dancing with gratitude for this moment of connection. Merric steadied himself against a column, overwhelmed by the depth of my response.

"After Casterbridge," Thomas began, his voice thick with memory's weight, "King Leofric was devastated. He had loved Edmund like a son. He brought him here, to rest in this garden where they'd spent countless hours in counsel." His weathered hand traced carved oak leaves that crowned the tomb. "When Malvora's shadow fell across our borders, Leofric's grief transformed to righteous fury. He led the army himself and brought King Burgund to his final accounting."

Thomas's face darkened like clouds before a storm. "But before Burgund's execution, the truth emerged. Prince Zevrin—Leofric's own son—had struck a devil's bargain. Burgund promised him Valandria's crown in exchange for drawing away Casterbridge's defenders."

Through our bond, I felt Merric's shock mirror my own. Edmund had always suspected someone had orchestrated the keep's abandonment, but to learn it was the prince himself—that betrayal ran deeper than any blade could reach.

"Leofric showed no mercy," Thomas continued. "He banished Zevrin, declaring that death awaited if he ever darkened our borders again. The crown passed to young Prince Alfred instead, and when Leofric joined Edmund in rest, Alfred proved himself his father's true heir. He rules with wisdom and compassion, as Edmund always believed a king should."

Standing there in morning light that painted everything gold, I felt weight lift from my essence—a question long carried finally finding its answer. Edmund's suspicions had been proven right. Justice, though delayed, had prevailed. I gazed upon the tomb of my dear friend and felt peace settle over me like a blessing from above.

"Thank you, Thomas," Merric spoke for both of us, his voice gentle. "For sharing this truth, and for keeping Edmund's memory alive."

The old squire bowed his head. "It has been my honor, these long years, to tend this garden in my spare time. To ensure that those who visit know not just of Edmund's death, but of how he lived—with courage, wisdom, and unfailing kindness."

As we turned to leave, I took one last look at the pavilion. In the growing light, it seemed to glow with its own inner radiance, a fitting tribute to the knight who had taught me so much about what it truly meant to serve.

* * *

After weeks of travel, we crested the final hill overlooking Thistlebrook. The village hadn't changed much in two hundred and fifty years—the same thatched roofs, the same stone well, the same apple orchards stretching toward sunset.

Stop here, I whispered into Merric's mind. *There's something you need to see.*

121

As his hand touched my hilt, I opened the memories. The prideful warrior strode through these same streets, my steel thirsting for blood at his command. His arrogance flowed through our connection—each victory feeding his belief that might made right.

I showed Merric how the warrior had terrorized the villagers, demanding taxes and obedience. Until that day when a humble swordsman passed through, carrying a simple blade and a servant's heart. Their duel lasted mere moments—skill and wisdom overcoming brute force and pride.

They buried him there, I shared, directing Merric's gaze to the spot beneath an ancient oak. *And left me upon his grave as a warning against pride's corruption. For seventy years, I waited, watching seasons change, until Elara found me.*

Warmth flooded through my essence as I recalled the healer's gentle touch. How she'd used me not as a weapon, but as a staff to support her travels. I showed Merric her quiet strength, her dedication to healing both body and spirit. The way she'd taught me that true power lies in protection, not destruction.

I had so much regret after all the lives I took in the warrior's hand, I confided. *Through Elara, I learned forgiveness, and how to eventually forgive myself.*

"You miss her," Merric observed softly.

I do. But now... home calls. My spirit flickered. *The place where I was born lies just a day's journey ahead.*

I felt Merric's concern as my power continued to fade. The divine light that had once blazed through my steel now burned low. We both knew my time grew short.

"Then we'll reach it tomorrow," Merric declared, his grip tightening around my hilt. "Together."

* * *

The morning sun painted the eastern sky gold as we rode through the ancient forests of Talinthor. My heart stirred at familiar scents—pine needles, mountain streams, and something deeper.

"We are now entering the kingdom of Talinthor, one of the most ancient kingdoms in the world," Roland announced with scholarly reverence.

I felt Merric's wonder surge. "I never thought I would have the opportunity to travel this far, to this special kingdom. Most of the world's ancient tales are woven from these very lands."

Thomas nodded sagely. "This kingdom has had its ups and downs but has stood the test of time."

Something pulled at my core, a sensation both foreign and achingly familiar. *It's close,* I whispered into Merric's mind. *I can feel it in my steel—home is near.*

As our party crested the hill, recognition surged through me. There, sprawling across the valley below, stood what had once been a modest town. Now Dunrowen had grown into a magnificent city, its spires reaching toward the heavens, its walls gleaming in the morning light.

That is the city I know, I shared through our bond. *Though it is bigger now, that is my home.*

"Dunrowen," Thomas breathed reverently. "The home of Sir Gregory, the greatest blacksmith to ever live, and Truthseeker, the greatest sword ever made."

The city streets teemed with life, so different from my memories. Where once stood humble wooden shops now towered stone buildings. Markets sprawled where gardens once bloomed, and paved roads replaced the dirt paths I had known.

I felt Merric's steady patience as I guided him through the maze of streets. More than once, I led us down what I remembered as a direct route, only to find new buildings blocking the way. I flickered with frustration until finally, a familiar landmark caught my attention—the old bell tower, its weathered stone still standing proud.

There, I whispered to Merric. *Turn left at the tower. The path should lead us...*

My thoughts trailed off as we rounded the corner. The narrow lane opened into a peaceful cemetery, exactly as I remembered it. Time seemed to slow as my spirit recognized this sacred ground. The cherry tree still stood sentinel over the graves, its pink blossoms dancing in the gentle breeze.

And there beneath it lay a sight that made my heart sing—Sir Gregory's tomb. Pure white marble gleamed in the filtered sunlight, and atop it lay a perfectly carved likeness of my creator. Every detail was captured in stone—his kind eyes, his strong hands, the gentle smile that had greeted me upon my first awakening. The tomb looked as though it had been carved yesterday, its surface unmarred by time.

A man stood beside the grave, carefully replacing wilted flowers with fresh blooms. His movements held reverence.

I urged Merric forward. He approached the man, removing a small loaf of fresh bread from his pack as an offering.

"Is this the final resting place of Sir Gregory?" Merric asked softly.

The man turned, accepting the bread with a gracious nod. His features held echoes of my creator—the same thoughtful eyes, the same strong jaw. "Indeed it is. This is the tomb of my ancestor."

Joy surged through my essence, nearly overwhelming my connection with Merric. Here stood a living link to the man who had given me life, who had infused me with purpose. Through all my centuries of wandering, I had never dared hope to find Sir Gregory's bloodline still flowing strong.

Merric's heart swelled with emotion as he watched the man tend to his ancestor's grave. A single tear traced down his weathered cheek, catching the morning light.

"Your name, good sir?" Merric asked quietly.

"Hugo," the man replied, straightening from his task.

Merric drew me from my scabbard with practiced grace. He presented me horizontally, my blade catching the filtered sunlight beneath the cherry blossom.

"It is my pleasure to share with you the last and greatest creation that Sir Gregory had made," Merric said. "This is the blade Truthseeker."

Hugo's eyes widened as he gazed upon my steel. His hand trembled slightly as he reached out, fingers brushing over the maker's mark Sir Gregory had lovingly etched into my crossguard. The moment his flesh touched the ancient sigil, I opened the floodgates of memory.

I showed him Sir Gregory's face, not carved in cold marble but alive with passion and purpose. The warmth of the forge surrounded us as Gregory worked, each hammer stroke infused with love and dedication. I shared the moment he breathed life into my steel, giving a piece of his own spirit that I might serve a greater purpose.

Hugo's knees buckled and he sank to the ground, clutching me to his chest as tears flowed freely down his face. Through our brief connection, I felt his joy and wonder at experiencing these precious moments—seeing the face of his legendary ancestor not in paintings or stone, but in living memory.

"Thank you, thank you," Hugo whispered, his voice thick with emotion. "To see his face is something I never thought would have been possible."

A voice called from behind us, warm and concerned. "Is everything okay, Hugo?"

Through my fading spirit, I recognized something in the young man's bearing—an echo of another soul I had known long ago.

"Elias, come and see, it is Truthseeker!" Hugo called out, his voice trembling with excitement.

Elias hurried forward, his strong hands bearing the calluses of a skilled craftsman. "I can't believe it," he breathed. "The blade my grandfather stole as a child…"

My essence surged with recognition. Kieran's grandson stood before me, carrying his grandfather's gentle spirit in his eyes. As his fingers brushed my hilt, memories flowed between us—Kieran teaching him the craft, sharing tales of a magical sword that had changed his life's path. I saw through Elias's memories how he had poured his heart into crafting Sir Gregory's tomb, honoring the maker of the blade his grandfather had spoken of with such reverence.

"When Hugo needed someone to craft the tomb," Elias explained softly, "I knew I had to be the one. Grandfather's stories… they shaped my life's work."

Hugo's voice cut gently through the moment. "What brings you all here now?"

I felt Merric's heart constrict as he swallowed hard. "Truthseeker desired to return home. His essence is nearly gone."

My friends, I spoke into all their minds, *I wish to rest with my creator.*

Hugo carefully handed me back to Merric, and I gathered my fading strength for one final farewell to the man who had carried me with such honor for over thirty years.

Merric, I whispered into his heart, *you showed me what it truly means to serve with purpose. Through you, I finally understood why Sir Gregory gave me life. Not to seek glory or power, but to help reveal the light within others. You never needed me to be a king—that greatness was always within your heart. I was merely the mirror that helped you see it.*

Tears flowed freely down Merric's cheeks as he held me one last time. "You were never just a sword," he whispered. "You were my truest friend, my wisest counselor, my constant companion through darkness and light."

And you were mine. Through you, I learned that even a blade can love, can grieve, can hope. Thank you, my dear friend, for helping me find my way home.

With infinite tenderness, Merric placed me in the empty stone hands of Sir Gregory's effigy. As I settled into my final rest, I felt complete—a circle closing, a journey ending where it began.

Through Sir Gregory's stone fingers, I gazed upward at the patches of blue sky visible through the cherry blossoms. The gentle breeze carried petals through the air, dancing like pink snowflakes around my friends. Their tears fell silently as my essence continued to fade, my steel slowly transforming to match the marble of the tomb beneath me.

Merric's quiet sobs echoed in my heart. Thomas stood rigid, a soldier's discipline warring with his grief. Hugo and Elias knelt beside the tomb, their shoulders shaking with emotion. Roland and Edgar clutched each other's arms, watching as I merged with Sir Gregory's tomb.

How I wished I could join them in their sorrow, to shed tears alongside these precious souls who had touched my existence in so many ways. As this thought filled my fading essence, a small grey cloud materialized in the clear sky above. Drops of rain began to fall, pattering against my steel like tears I could never shed on my own.

My heart swelled with gratitude. Even in these final moments, the great Creator showed His tender mercy, allowing me this one last gift—the ability to weep with those I loved. Each raindrop that struck my blade felt like a prayer of thanksgiving for all the lives I had been privileged to touch, all the truths I had helped reveal.

With the last remnants of my voice, I spoke aloud to my gathered friends: "I leave you with this, my dear friends—seek truth in all you do, seek it above all else, for truth will never lead you astray."

THE END

About the Author

You can connect with me on:

🌐 https://www.jacobsansoucie.com

f https://www.facebook.com/jsansoucie.author

Subscribe to my newsletter:

✉ https://www.jacobsansoucie.com

www.ingramcontent.com/pod-product-compliance
Lightning Source LLC
Chambersburg PA
CBHW072030170626
46811CB00008B/3009